The

GRAVE
TENDER

ALSO BY ELIZA MAXWELL

The Kinfolk

The

GRAVE

TENDER

ELIZA MAXWELL

This is a work of fiction. Names, characters, organizations, places, events, and incidents are either products of the author's imagination or are used fictitiously. Any resemblance to actual persons, living or dead, or actual events is purely coincidental.

Published by Lake Union Publishing, Seattle
www.apub.com

Amazon, the Amazon logo, and Lake Union Publishing are trademarks of Amazon.com, Inc., or its affiliates.

ISBN-13: 9781477818473
ISBN-10: 1477818472

Cover design by David Drummond

Printed in the United States of America

For my mom,
who taught me that
crazy only counts
if it shows

1

It was a mother's coldest fear. In the space where her three-year-old son should have been, Hadley Dixon found nothing but air.

A quick search of his bedroom revealed only the stars and rocket ship painted on the wall and scattered toys on the floor, giving no hints. She checked his sister's room. Sometimes he liked to play there, a dragon hoarding his treasure in a cave under the bed. Nothing but dust.

She searched the rest of the farmhouse, her footsteps echoing across the worn wooden floorboards. Nothing.

"Charlie!" She called his name into quiet rooms. The silence screamed back at her.

The hundred-year-old house replied to her cries with a bang of the screen door, caught by the wind. It was loud. Too loud.

Hadley whipped around and saw the front door ajar, just a crack. But enough. Enough to let the outside in. Enough to let a little boy out.

For the briefest moment of time, she stared. Then panic broke over her.

She ran, pulling the oak front door wide and bursting past the screen door that slammed against the side of the house in protest. She flew into the brightness of the day.

Hadley turned, her eyes flitting across the landscape, lush with spring. The gardenias' first green buds, the nest of baby sparrows crying from the front eave. Life all around her, mocking her useless, empty arms.

"Charlie! Charlie!"

She turned faster, the tall pines spinning by.

"Charlie!"

The barn. Maybe he was there, with the horses. He liked it there, among the broken animals with their flecked paint and golden poles. But the door was shut. Even as she raised the wooden bar and pulled the door open with a creak of old hinges, Hadley knew she wouldn't find him there. Light played on the dust particles floating in the air. Only the horses, whose expressions and gaits hadn't changed since they'd been created. He was nowhere. He was gone.

Hadley forced herself to slow, to listen, to see.

But it made no difference. Only the silence of the horses and the hollow wind filled her ears.

The hour and a half that followed was a walk across broken glass. Every terrible possibility cut, exposing flesh and bone.

By the time searchers, hastily called in a breathless void of coherency, spotted the boy walking hand in hand with Mrs. Abbott, Hadley had run the bloody gauntlet of loss.

Voices shouted for her, and she turned, her breath caught in the space between her heart and her throat, certain they were bringing her the body of her son, dead because of her. Because of her lies. Because of her sins.

"Mama!" Charlie cried. He looked surprised to see her but pleased by the chance meeting.

Hadley ran to him, then lifted her son into her arms, overwhelmed by the damp, sweet scent of boy. Tears rolled down her face, soaking into her son's tousled, sweaty curls.

The people surrounding them were speaking. She didn't hear any of it. Not the relieved sighs of *Thank God* or the explanations of how

Mrs. Abbott had discovered an unexpected visitor laughing in delight as he fed wildflowers into her bunny hutch.

Hadley turned her eyes upward. There, watching them with reflective black eyes, was a line of crows perched, one after another, on the wire that stretched from one utility pole to the next.

How many crows does it take to make a murder, she wondered. She squeezed her eyes closed, blocking their watchful gaze.

It didn't matter, Hadley thought. Crows be damned. It was the sins of her family, and her own, that had come home to roost. Huge hook-beaked birds that fed on carrion. They'd taken her son, then brought him back. To show they could. As a warning. A long time ago, there'd been another boy. One who hadn't made it back.

Hadley held her child close. She had a great deal to answer for.

2

Hadley had watched her daddy steal a boy back from death once. That was the hope she held tight while she ran, sneakers slapping the earth, her hair whipping around her face.

Daddy could fix it. She knew he could.

It had happened last summer, during a birthday party at the reservoir. Walker had come to collect Hadley. No one noticed when the boy's head sank beneath the water without a sound. No one but Walker Dixon.

One moment, he was listening with half a smile while she tried to talk him into just five more minutes. In the next, he was sprinting past her to the water, kicking off his shoes. Hadley could only watch, openmouthed. It wasn't until she heard the other adults begin to count heads and shout for their children that she realized someone had gone under.

The kids were pulled out of the water by anxious parents. They stood dripping in soggy suits that clung to them while more adults waded in to help Walker. He was diving, searching for any sign of the child.

Hadley let out a pent-up breath each time he surfaced, then held it again when he dived back into the muddy water. Her lungs burned and her chest cried for air, but she knew if she gave in, if she couldn't hold that breath, then neither could he, and his head would never break the surface.

And then he came up one last time, the boy in his arms. Hadley's legs went out from beneath her and she sucked in air, pushing out the terror. The parents and kids lined up along the bank gave a quick cheer, but it soon gave way to silence again.

Walker had found the boy, but he wasn't breathing, his head rolling on his shoulders. Mothers pulled their children to them, holding them close and hiding their eyes while her daddy came out of the water with a dead child in his arms.

There was no one to cover Hadley's eyes. She watched as her father laid the boy on the sandy shore, then took a finger and cleared the dirt and muddy water out of the boy's mouth, turning his head to the side.

It was Teddy Benoit. He was in Hadley's class.

Walker positioned his hands on the boy's skinny chest.

Teddy sat three desks behind her.

Walker pushed.

Teddy played baseball at the park with the other boys after school. Third base.

Walker pushed again.

Teddy was learning the guitar. His granddad was teaching him. He'd brought the guitar to school once for show-and-tell. He wasn't very good, and he knew it, but his granddad said he would be one day. So he was going to practice.

Walker pinched the boy's nostrils closed and leaned down, breathing air into the boy's lungs.

Teddy said he'd bring the guitar back, after he practiced. After he was good, and they'd all see how much better he'd gotten.

Walker breathed into the boy's lungs a second time.

Teddy would never get any better. He was dead, with mud smeared across his shins, under the brutal east Texas sun with his friends standing silently over him.

Everyone knew it except for Walker, who moved to push at the boy's chest again.

It was too late for Teddy to get any better. Not at the guitar, not at anything.

Teddy coughed. Then he turned and vomited water and mucus onto the ground. Everyone let out the breath locked in their chests.

Within days, Teddy Benoit was back to playing ball and cutting up in class. And now Hadley needed her daddy again.

Slamming the front door open, she skidded to a halt just inside.

"Daddy!" she cried.

Chairs scraped in the kitchen, where Walker was having a cup of coffee with his mother, her grandma Alva, before work. He was a general contractor, and his company was working a big job in Cordelia. He'd been leaving early and coming home late all month. She was lucky to catch him home. "Hadley, baby, what's the matter? Are you hurt?" he asked.

She shook her head, out of breath.

"No," she managed, then sucked in enough air to say, "Daddy, you gotta come quick. The bus stop."

Walker wasted no time, racing after her as she took off running back the way she'd come, launching herself off the front steps and down the quarter-mile driveway to where the big yellow bus picked up her and a handful of other kids for school. When they got there, the others were huddled in a circle.

"No, don't touch her," she heard Jo Jo say.

"I'm just gonna hold her head, so she isn't afraid," Jude said, using her big sister tone.

"Back up now, kids," Walker said, gently moving them out of the way.

"Oh, thank Christ," Hadley heard him whisper when he caught a glimpse of the figure on the ground.

"But, Daddy—" she started. He held up a hand in her direction, cutting her off.

He knelt and looked at each of the children gathered there. Jude Monroe and two of her younger brothers, Jo Jo and Mikey, and Cooper Abbott from across the road.

"Are any of you kids hurt?" he asked.

They all shook their heads.

"We found her like this, Mr. Dixon. Can you help her?" Jude asked. She held the head of a small black-and-white-spotted dog in her lap.

The yellow bus came chugging around the corner, coughing fumes and leaving dust in its wake.

Walker nodded at the kids, then began to unbutton his shirt, revealing the white T-shirt he wore beneath. As the bus came to a stop with a screech of brakes, he gathered up the little dog's broken body into his shirt.

None of the kids made a move.

"Y'all go on now and get to school," Walker said, and they reluctantly began moving toward the waiting door of the bus. All but Hadley.

"Daddy, can't I just stay with you?" Hadley asked.

"No, ma'am. You get your butt on that bus," Walker said.

Hadley's forehead wrinkled and she opened her mouth, but he shook his head before she could get started.

"Hadley, I promise you, I'll do what I can to help this dog, but your place is at school," he said softly. "Now go on. Ms. Hatcher isn't gonna wait all day."

Hadley glanced over her shoulder at the bus driver, whose usual surly disposition was only slightly tempered by Walker's presence.

"Sorry for the holdup, Betty. She's coming," he called.

Ms. Hatcher's lacquered, rust-colored curls moved with her head when she nodded in his direction. Her chins had more freedom and jiggled at the movement.

"Get a move on, then, girl," she said. Hadley gave up, knowing when she was beat. Taking the three large steps onto the bus in leaps, she moved to her seat next to Jude. They watched Walker wave to

Ms. Hatcher, then head back toward home, moving carefully with the bundle cradled in his arms.

The lumbering bus choked out some more fumes and carried them away.

All day the girls worried about the dog. Had she lived? Would her legs have to be cut off the way Mr. Sayers's had been when he was hurt in Vietnam? Mr. Sayers had a wheelchair that he always parked in front of the Rainbow Café, where he drank free coffee and spit tobacco juice into a Coke can. They discussed it at length but eventually agreed a wheelchair for dogs was unlikely.

After school they bolted from the steps of the school bus and ran all the way back to Hadley's house. They'd spotted Walker's truck out front and knew he'd be there somewhere with news of the dog's fate. The screen door slammed, announcing their arrival.

"Daddy, Daddy, where's the dog?" Hadley asked, out of breath. She found her father in the little room just off the living room that he used for an office. Jude was right behind her. "Is she okay, Mr. Dixon? Did she die? If she died, we should have a funeral for her. We can wear all black and sing some sad hymns and invite everyone. My grandpa's funeral was packed with people, and he didn't even get hit by a car. Actually, Mama says he wasn't a very nice man, but she doesn't say that in front of Daddy, because it was his daddy and he doesn't like to talk about him much, even though he's dead now and can't be mean to anybody anymore anyway."

Jude paused for a breath. Hadley took over in a slightly calmer tone.

"Daddy, Jude and I can take care of her together. She can go back and forth between our houses. That way neither of us is taking on too much responsibility." It was a good argument. Daddy and Gran were always going on about responsibility.

Jude stepped up to the plate. "Hadley wants to name her Elizabeth after the Queen of England, but that seems too stuffy to me. What does a beat-up old dog in Whitewood, Texas, know about England? I think we should call her Lucky, but Hadley says she wasn't very lucky when that car hit her, unless bad luck counts. But Bad Lucky isn't a very good name for a dog either."

"Whoa, girls," Walker said. "Slow down there."

The girls froze, eyes wide. Bending down on one knee, he took one of each of their hands in his.

"The dog is still alive," he told them, "but she's in pretty bad shape. She may need to be put down." Jude opened her mouth, probably to say something about doggie wheelchairs, but Walker shushed her with a look.

"It's very compassionate of you girls to want to help a stray like that. I'd say her luck took a turn for the better when you two found her just as she needed a helping hand . . . But," he said. Hadley hated it when he said *but* that way. "There's a good chance she's not gonna make it. Even if she does, dressing wounds and caring for injured animals is no job for ten-year-olds, as responsible as you two may be."

He shook his head when they opened their mouths to protest.

"Uh-uh. I've taken her over to my brother Eli's place. He'll be able to do whatever needs to be done. Now you girls run along to the kitchen. My nose is telling me your grandmother did some baking today, so why don't you go see what you can wheedle out of her?"

Walker herded them out of his office, paying no notice to their faces, mirror images of horror.

"To your uncle Eli's place?! But, but . . . he's so scary and weird! And scary. I mean, I know he's your uncle and all, but still . . ." Jude trailed off.

Hadley didn't say anything. Daddy and Gran said Eli was harmless, but she'd heard the whispers around town. He frightened people with his scarred face and strange, quiet ways. He frightened her. Eli was always lurking in the shadows, always at the edges of her life. There were only a few dark places in her safe, secure world, and the blackest of those was her uncle Eli. Even Mama's crazy didn't compare. That was ordinary crazy. Eli, though—that was different. What was Daddy think-ing, sending a wounded animal to Eli in that little shack by the river? There was no electricity, no running water. Worse still were the trees. Eli's carved trees that peppered the woods. Living things with eyes that never closed. Her father told her Eli lived out there by choice. It was a choice she couldn't wrap her head around.

Others said Eli Dixon had been damaged by a bad childhood, and now he was broken beyond what could be fixed. But her father had shared a childhood with Eli, and he was okay. She didn't know much about her grandfather Silas. He'd run off before she was born, back when the Dixon farm included the surrounding land, before it had all been sold off or leased to other farmers. They didn't harvest rice anymore. The only farming they did was Gran's little plot that put tomatoes, squash, and jalapeños on their table every year. Her favorite, though, were the dewberries that grew wild on the riverbank. Those her grandmother didn't bother to cultivate. They grew like weeds every spring, low bushes full of stickers and thorns. Picking dewberries left you with scratched, stinging arms—it was worth it for Gran's berry cobbler. But Hadley flat refused to pick berries by the river alone. The one time she had was something she wouldn't soon forget.

It was a dark, tangled corner of the woods, a place she'd normally not venture into. But the berries were fat and ripe, dripping from the bushes.

She could feel the trees watching her. The carvings were thick there. She knew they weren't real. Knew the owl with the fierce dead eyes wasn't going to fly out with his wooden wings beating and attack her. Knew that the face of the man caught in a scream couldn't grab her and pull her in.

So she told herself.

Still, she moved quickly, keeping her eyes on her nervous, purple-stained fingers.

"Not those. Not for you, girl." Hadley had stood up and whipped around so quickly that her feet had gotten tangled. She fell backward into the brambles, crying out at the sudden, sharp pain. It was Eli. He was running awkwardly toward her, bumbling with his big clumsy body. He looked angry, his face painted with scars and a wildness in his eyes that made her think one of his carvings had come to life. Hadley panicked, her bucket of berries forgotten along with the bloody scratches on her hands and legs. Fear took over, and she stumbled to her feet, earning more scratches along the way. Then she ran.

She ran back home, escaping her uncle and those faces in the woods. Her heart hammered in her chest. Even after she had slammed herself into her room, it took a painfully long time for her skin to stop prickling. Hadley had never told a soul, not even Jude. It was hard to find the words to describe the sense of wrongness she felt from her uncle. If Hadley couldn't explain it to herself, she knew she'd never make another person understand. She didn't even try.

But the thought of that poor dog trapped with her uncle knotted Hadley's stomach up. Maybe Bad Lucky wasn't such a bad name after all.

3

That night, Hadley walked up the stairs to her mama's room, running her hand along the bannister as she went. The aged, oiled wood was smooth under her fingers. She loved this house, when she slowed down enough to think about it. It was a member of the family, part of who they were.

Nestled into a curve in the woods that ran along the Neches River, the place had an air of timelessness. A weathered grace that said, *I've seen it all, and I can handle whatever you've got, kid, so come on in and make yourself at home.*

Hadley knocked lightly on her mama's door.

"Come in," Winnie called over the sound of the radio. It was tuned to the country station out of Cordelia, and her mother was singing along. Hadley opened the door and entered her mama's world.

Winnie was sitting at her vanity, massaging cream into her cheeks.

"Hadley, honey," she said. "You're just in time to help me set my hair." Winnie's reflection smiled at her in the mirror, and Hadley knew it had been a good day.

"Sure, Mama," Hadley said, and pulled up a stool so she could take the two-inch rollers out of Winnie's hair. She loved to watch the auburn curls bounce out of their rollers, soft and loose, before Winnie teased them up and froze them in place with her big blue can of hairspray.

"It'll be a packed house tonight, darlin'," Winnie said, her eyes shining.

"Standing room only," Hadley said, as she let down her mother's curls, one by one.

There were a lot of things Hadley tried not to take for granted. Simple things.

Gran said Winnie hadn't always been this way, but she had been for as long as Hadley could remember, so that meant little to her. Occasionally, she wondered if it was an inherited thing, something that would come up on her all of a sudden. If she'd wake up one morning with the crazies, like the red welts that came with the chicken pox she'd had when she was five. But most days Hadley didn't worry about it. Winnie didn't leave the house much. Or ever, really, except to wander the woods by the river at night. People in town said she was a bit touched and shook their heads for the little girl being brought up with a mama like that. Hadley ran her hands through her mother's hair. She knew Mama loved her, in her own way.

When Winnie was on an upswing, she and Daddy would dance in the kitchen on bare feet.

"Come on, Hadley," Walker would say and grab her in a spin, pulling her into their circle.

It wasn't always bad. But as the years picked up speed, Winnie had drifted farther and farther away from the world, until only a fragile web kept her feet bound to the earth and her family.

The crazy came and went. For months at a time, things were almost normal. And if, in the middle of the night, while the rest of the house slept, Hadley sometimes woke to the haunting sounds of a voice coming from the pines, singing old blues songs about loss and pain and grief, well, it could have been worse.

But then, without warning, things would come unspooled. Winnie's songs turned to silence and she'd lock herself in her room for days. Hadley's room was below her mother's. She'd hear her pacing the floorboards at night. Sometimes it sounded like Mama was praying.

Sometimes she cried, as if a billion tiny knives were cutting her open from the inside.

That was bad.

But nothing was worse than the screaming.

On the screaming nights, Walker went through his wife's bedroom door and held Winnie tight while she screamed like the fires of hell were surrounding her. Maybe they were.

Once Winnie's beautiful voice was ripped up and her body was drained, she'd give in to exhaustion, the silence stretching tight as a wire.

When Walker would emerge from her room, his eyes red from crying tears of his own, Hadley was sure he'd somehow found a way to take all Winnie's pain into himself, leaving his wife empty and spent. But it came back the next day to fill her up again. It always came back.

Shaking off the melancholy thoughts, Hadley hugged her mama, then kissed her cheek.

"Good night, Mama."

Winnie smiled vaguely at her daughter and ran a hand down Hadley's hair.

"Night, love," she said, then turned back to the mirror and the task at hand.

It wasn't much, maybe, but as Hadley let herself out of her mama's room, closing the door on the powdery scents and twangy music, she was grateful it wasn't a screaming night.

These things were all she'd ever known. She didn't spend a lot of time asking herself why her mother was the way she was. She just was.

4

It was called recess but felt more like punishment.

The kids of Mrs. Huffman's fourth-grade class claimed any available shade. But shade couldn't do anything about the humidity that made the air too thick to breathe.

It was October. Heat-weary, the residents of east Texas waited for summer to give up and die, but it held on like a leech, sucking the life out of the place, getting fat.

To pass the time, the girls daydreamed of Halloween, candy, and, more important, a crisp, cool fall that was still weeks away.

"I could be the (*slap*) Lone Ranger and you (*slap*) could be Tonto."

"Why am I (*slap*) the side (*slap*) kick?" *Slap, slap.*

The sharp sound of playing cards punctuated the exchange, lending a strange staccato rhythm.

"Because it was my idea, (*slap*) and besides, I'm black." *Slap.*

Jude waited for Hadley to throw out the next card. When it didn't come, she looked up at her friend's bemused expression.

"What?" she asked.

Hadley shook her head. "What does that have to do with anything?"

"Well, I can't be *your* sidekick. It'd make you look like a racist cracker. So you have to be mine."

"I'm not a racist!" She didn't argue the cracker part.

"I know, but think about how it'd look."

"That's stupid. Besides, you're only half black. When Mrs. Huffman chose parts for the play, you got Pocahontas because you told her you're Indian."

"So? I am Indian. My nana on my mama's side is full-blooded Choctaw." *Slap*.

"Maybe so, but you can't pick and choose whenever it suits you."

"Course I can. I'm not lying, am I? My nana's Choctaw, my mama's Creole, and my daddy's black. Just the way it is."

An image of Joseph Monroe flashed through Hadley's mind. He was laughing. He was always laughing.

"Your daddy's full of horseshit, is what he is."

"True enough," Jude said. *Slap*. "But he's still black. Not my fault your whole family's plain old vanilla."

Next to Jude, with her gold-dust skin, Hadley looked like a coloring page that someone had forgotten to color in. All pale skin and dark hair, with eyes a little too big for her face. Another kind of girl might have been jealous. Even at ten, everybody knew Jude was destined for beauty. But the girls had been friends too long for that, their faces as familiar to one another as an old pair of shoes. And the appeal of male attention was only a distant specter somewhere in the fog of someday, maybe.

Slap.

"I win," Jude announced, scooping up the deck of cards.

"Tonto was an Indian," Hadley pointed out.

"Yeah," Jude said. "But it's Halloween. You be the Indian, and I'll be the cracker in a white cowboy suit."

"Stop calling me a cracker."

"I'm not calling you a cracker."

"Not this time, but you just did."

"I said that's what people'd say! I'm trying to do you a favor."

"Just hand 'em over. I'll shuffle," Hadley said.

There was no point in arguing. She kind of liked the idea of dressing up as Tonto. But she wasn't telling Jude that.

As Hadley deftly handled the worn deck of cards, her ears pricked up at a sound drifting across the schoolyard. Glancing at Jude, she saw her friend's nose lift and her head turn.

Without a word, the girls were up and running, the playing cards abandoned in the dirt. Before they'd made two steps, they heard the universal battle cry of savage children everywhere.

"Fight!"

A crowd had gathered by the time they pushed their way into the circle, the chant of *fight, fight, fight* filling the air.

Hadley could make out little more than limbs and sneakers rolling around in the dirt.

"It's Cooper," Jude said in her ear, trying to be heard over the din.

"That's no surprise," Hadley said, craning and shoving to see around the bigger kids.

"And Sam!" Jude said.

"Sam?"

Sam Brooks and Cooper Abbott were friends, but you wouldn't know it, the way they were pounding on each other. Sam seemed, at first, to have the upper hand, but even as she thought it, Hadley saw Cooper land an elbow to the bigger boy's eye, then break free as Sam tried to pin him down.

Scrambling to his feet, Cooper ran straight at Hadley, who'd managed to push her way to the front of the crowd.

"Hey!" she shouted, as Cooper grabbed her shoulders and positioned himself behind her, using her as a shield. For all his swagger, he wasn't much bigger than she was.

Grinning, Cooper laughed. "Help me out here—he won't hit you."

Sam came toward them. His eye was starting to swell.

"That's chickenshit, Coop," he sneered. "Hiding behind a little girl."

"Who you calling little, Sam Brooks?" Hadley asked. Cooper was ducking and weaving behind her with a grin on his face.

Sam, who'd shot up almost a foot over the summer, had to lean down a bit to look Hadley in the eye. "You, shrimp."

Ever since Hadley was little, she'd had a temper that ran deep and low. It didn't show itself much. But her daddy said he could see when it was about to break through. Her face would get rigid, her nostrils flaring, just before it reared up. He called it her ox face.

Jude saw it coming. Sam didn't.

Not until a pale, bony fist flashed, connecting with the nose he'd unwisely placed within her reach.

Blood spurted, Jude gasped, Sam howled in pain, and over it all, Cooper's manic laughter rang like calliope music at the fair.

"Hadley Dixon!" The strident tone of Mrs. Huffman gave away her irritation at being forced to cut her conversation with Coach Bagley short. The two were presumably monitoring their young charges, but there had been heavy flirting happening, and she wasn't a happy woman.

Hadley's ear was wrenched in the teacher's grasp, and where your ear goes, so goes the rest of you. She was dragged off toward the principal's office.

"But, Mrs. Huffman, I didn't—"

"Hush it, young lady. I don't want to hear about what you didn't do. I saw you punch that boy in the nose."

She called back over her shoulder, ear still firmly in her grip, "You too, Mr. Brooks. First to the nurse's office; then the principal will want a word with you as well."

Sam trailed sullenly behind them, his hands still on his nose. Jude watched them go, but the rest of the onlookers had scattered to the winds at the first sign of authority, including Cooper Abbott, who'd no doubt started the whole thing.

Hadley was sitting on a bench outside Mr. Gilmore's office when she saw her father walking up the hall.

"Daddy, I—"

He held up a hand. "You'll get your turn, but not yet," he said, taking in the sight of Sam sitting silently next to her, drops of dried blood marring the collar of his T-shirt.

The two kids hadn't spoken, and didn't still, while they waited for Mr. Dixon to come out of the principal's office.

When the door finally opened, Hadley kept her eyes on the floor. Walker squatted in front of her and waited for her to meet his gaze.

"Your turn, Hadley. Did you punch this boy?"

She'd had so much she planned to say, but her indignation evaporated under her father's stern eyes.

She nodded.

"Did he hit you first?"

Hadley saw Sam stiffen beside her, listening, but he stayed silent.

She thought for a moment about lying but knew she couldn't. Not to her daddy. Not with Sam sitting there taking in every word.

"No, Daddy," she said.

"Why'd you hit him, Hadley?"

"He . . . he called me little."

Walker's eyebrows arched.

"He called you little?" he asked, and Hadley could hear how ridiculous that sounded.

"Yes, Daddy."

"Hadley Dixon," Walker said, shaking his head. "I hate to break it to you, girl, but you are little. At least on the outside."

He stood.

"Apologize to Mr. Brooks."

She whipped her eyes upward, but there was no give in her daddy's face. With a long-suffering sigh, she turned to Sam, knowing her father would expect her to do it right.

"I'm sorry I punched you in the nose, Sam," she said. "I hope your mama can get the stains out of your shirt."

Sam looked down and quickly mumbled, "'S alright."

Hadley could tell he wanted this whole thing over nearly as bad as she did.

With a nod to Sam, Walker held out a hand for Hadley to take, and that was that.

Except for the switching she got once they arrived home.

5

The next day Hadley stayed close to her room. Her butt, as well as her pride, was still sore.

Midmorning, Gran knocked on her door, then came inside carrying a stack of laundry. Tossing aside her sketchbook, Hadley rose to help her put it away. For a moment, the two worked in concert, under the hum of the ceiling fan.

"Your daddy said he's thinking of driving into Cordelia today," Gran said.

Under normal circumstances, Hadley would have jumped up, run down the stairs immediately, and pestered her father to let her tag along. Cordelia was the closest thing to a real city in fifty miles, much bigger than Whitewood and infinitely more interesting. Instead, she bit her lip.

"Probably enjoy the company," Gran said, her back to her granddaughter as she put a stack of socks away in the dresser drawer.

"You don't think he's still mad at me?"

Gran's smile was soft when she turned and ran a hand down Hadley's hair.

"Your daddy was never mad at you, honey."

"You really don't think he'd mind?"

"What I think is that if he wanted to go alone, he would have left, instead of making a point of telling me his plans just as I was heading up the stairs, then fiddle-farting around in the kitchen over another cup of coffee he doesn't need."

Hadley grinned.

"Now get a move on, before he gets tired of waiting on you to make up your mind."

"Can we stop at the bookstore before we go home?" Hadley asked, licking the ice cream that was creeping down her cone, making a sticky path toward her hand.

Walker ruffled her hair. "You think it's your birthday or something?"

Hadley shook her head but held out hope. A book was usually an easy sell, and it'd been a good day. No mention of yesterday's events. If she let herself, she could almost pretend it hadn't happened. Until she sat down.

"Not today." Walker ruffled her hair as she tried, and failed, to hide her disappointment.

"I have something else in mind."

The fat tubes lay side by side in their tray. There were sixteen of them, untouched and full of promise. Each one was marked with a saturated hue, like a badge of rank from a faraway place. *Vermilion, burnt umber, ultramarine.* Even the words felt exotic. Elegant, like red, orange, and blue, but all grown up and dressed for the opera.

"But . . . my art teacher . . . we haven't gotten that far. He said I need to master the basics of form and perspective before I start with paint."

Walker rolled his eyes.

"Hadley, sometimes it's okay to take a chance. The world is full of color, ladybug. Reach out and grab some of it."

Walker winked, and Hadley's head was suddenly reeling at the possibilities. She felt like she had when the training wheels had come off her bike, thrilled at the idea that she could move faster and farther than before.

"All I ask is that you put your heart into this. And not into handing out bloody noses."

Hadley realized that nothing had been forgotten. She hugged the paints to her chest, chastised, even as a whole new world waited in that little box.

6

"I don't understand what we're doing."

"I told you, I'm looking for the right subject."

"But why do *I* have to be here? I don't want to watch you paint. That's boring," Jude said.

"I'm not going to paint the whole thing, just sketch it out."

"But—"

"Hey, wait up!" Jude and Hadley turned to see Cooper running across the field toward them. Sam trailed behind at a slower pace. The Abbotts lived just across the gravel road from the Dixons, the nearest neighbors to Jude's family. Because of the way it was situated between their own houses, the two girls passed by Cooper's house daily, and they all caught the bus together, but Cooper didn't make a habit of seeking them out. They were girls.

The two waited at the edge of the woods that lined the river, but when Cooper caught up to them he leaned his hands on his knees, trying to catch his breath.

"Use your inhaler, dipshit. Everybody knows you have asthma," Sam said as he joined them. His eye had turned an interesting shade of purple, but his nose seemed to have recovered. Hadley wondered what paints she could mix to make that exact shade, but she looked away when Sam caught her staring.

Cooper fished his inhaler out of his pocket and sucked in two quick puffs, then quickly put it away.

"What are you guys doing?" he asked, once his breathing had calmed.

"You ran all the way over here to ask us that?" Jude said.

"Yep."

Hadley looked at Sam again, but he just shoved his hands in his pockets and shrugged. "We're going down by the river. Hadley's going to paint. It'll be boring," Jude replied, dismissing the boys and turning toward the path into the trees.

"You're not afraid old Meat Face is going to get you?" Cooper asked.

"Don't call him that," Hadley said, the reply automatic.

Cooper shrugged. "Sorry," he said. He didn't sound sorry. "But aren't you?"

She was. That's why she'd forced Jude to come along.

"Nah," Hadley said. "He stays over on the other side of his cabin."

Eli wandered wherever he liked.

"We'll come too."

"We will?" Sam asked.

"Suit yourself," Hadley said, pretending indifference.

Four was safer than two.

❧

". . . then the fisherman's wife demanded he go back to the river, catch the golden fish again, and wish that she would be the queen of everything she could see, including the river, so she could rule over the golden fish."

Hadley listened with half an ear. She'd heard the story before. It was one of Dr. Monroe's.

"But the golden fish was tired of granting wishes for the greedy old woman, so instead he turned her palace back into a shack and her fancy clothes back into rags. 'Enough is enough,' he said, and with a swish of his golden tail, he was gone."

"Why didn't the fisherman wish for something for himself?" Cooper asked. Jude and the two boys were chucking rocks into the river, its waters lazy in the heat. It was a pretty spot, where the trees stood back and let the sun shine in. There were no carvings here.

"Don't know," Jude said.

"'Cause he loved his wife, I guess," Hadley added, finishing up her sketch. She'd add the paint at home.

"I'd have wished for a different wife," said Sam.

"No way—" Cooper said, but Sam cut him off.

"Shh. You guys hear that?"

They stilled. At first, Hadley didn't hear anything save the water rolling by and the leaves doing their dance in the wind. Then there it was. The faint but unmistakable *crunch, slide* of a shovel.

It was coming from somewhere inside the shadowy thicket of trees farther up the river. Somewhere in the direction of Eli Dixon's shack.

"Come on, let's go see," Cooper whispered.

Jude shook her head. "I'm not going in there."

"What's the matter? You scared?" Cooper's eyes had taken on the familiar shine of a troublemaker.

"Yeah, I am," Jude said. "If you were smart, you'd be scared too."

"Stay here then, or go back," Cooper said, without malice. "But I want to see." And with a grin, he was off, moving toward the dense shade of the trees. Within seconds, he was gone.

"He's crazy," Hadley said, with grudging admiration.

"He's an idiot," Sam replied. "Come on, I'll walk you guys up to the house, then come back and find him."

"No," Hadley said, dumping her sketchbook and pencils in Jude's arms. "I'll go. Jude, you go back with Sam." They were both shaking their heads, but she stood her ground.

"I know where I'm going. You don't," she said to Sam, turning to follow Cooper.

"You're crazy too!" she heard Jude hiss softly behind her.

Somewhere up ahead, they heard the sound of a shovel biting into the earth.

Hadley motioned for her friends to get going, then let the shadows fall around her as she stepped into the trees.

When she found Cooper he was belly down, peering through a brushy clump of undergrowth, his bright strawberry-blond head a beacon, even in the shadows. She tried to stay quiet as she made her way toward him, but leaves rustled under her feet. He turned and held an urgent finger to his lips when a twig snapped.

Hadley wondered that he couldn't hear the drumbeat in her chest as she lay down next to him. He pointed up ahead and mouthed, "Look."

She peered through the brush. Eli's shack could barely be made out in the distance. You could hardly call it a home. It balanced precariously on cinder blocks, tilting slightly to one side, like an old drunk who'd given up the fight.

Her eyes adjusted to the dim light, but she still had to follow her ears to see what Cooper was gesturing at. The *crunch, slide* of the shovel was louder here, within the walls of the trees surrounding them. Hadley shivered at the sound.

Cooper leaned in to whisper, "Thanks for not tossing me in it with Gilmore."

She stared at him, openmouthed.

"Another mark, he'll suspend me. That was cool. You're pretty cool . . . for a girl," he added.

Up ahead, Eli slid his shovel into the ground next to him and stopped to wipe his brow. Seeing him brought the stifling heat to the forefront of Hadley's mind, and she had to fight the urge to wipe the sweat from her own face. Her nerve endings were singing, and she felt each drop as it trickled down her neck.

As the pair watched, Hadley's uncle leaned down and picked up a bundle, then knelt and placed the bundle into the hole he'd been digging. He took up the shovel again and threw a mound of dark earth back into the hole. They could hear the dirt spatter across whatever it was he'd placed down there.

Two pairs of wide eyes met. Cooper whispered, "It's a grave!"

"I know you're there." Eli's voice cut across the distance between them.

He didn't pause as he continued to shovel dirt into the waiting hole, covering the bundle below.

But Hadley and Cooper didn't see that. They were running, as fast and as far as the blood pumping in their veins would take them.

Hadley found her grandmother in the barn, with a carousel horse set into the pedestal by her worktable. This one had an empty look to it. The ones like that didn't bother Hadley so much.

It was the others, with their manes and tails flying behind them, even without the wind, that got to her. The ones with bits caught in their teeth and determination on their faces.

It was as if they knew they were destined to run on the same track forever—up, down, and around. They'd be stuck in a loop while laughing children walked away with cotton candy and a future.

"Gran, what happened to the dog?" Hadley asked.

Her grandmother's hands stalled, then she put down the brush she'd been using to clean the decades of grime from the creases in the horse's saddle.

She looked over the top of her glasses at Hadley.

"Your father didn't tell you?" she asked.

Hadley shook her head.

"She didn't make it, hon."

Gran watched her, waiting. Hadley nodded.

"Okay" was all she said. Hadley turned away, leaving her grand-mother to the care of a pretend horse that didn't know enough to know it wasn't real.

7

"I'm concerned, Walker. Her grip on reality has always been shaky at best, but this . . ." Dr. Monroe's voice was low as he and Walker crossed the porch, but he changed tack entirely when he caught sight of Hadley with her paints and easel set up at the far corner of the wraparound.

"Hey there, Hadley-bean. You doing okay today?"

"Yes, sir, Dr. Monroe."

"You sure? There's a mean virus going around. Serious, too. The way I hear it, it can turn skinny little white girls into heavyweight champs, just like that," he said with a snap of his fingers. "You're positive you're not coming down with any symptoms?"

Hadley shook her head, sheepishly casting a glance at her father, but he looked troubled and distant.

"Okay, if you're sure." Dr. Monroe continued down the porch steps, and Walker walked him down the drive. Hadley watched the two men shake hands, but she could make out little of what they said.

". . . needs to be soon . . . few days at most . . . sorry, Walker."

Then Dr. Monroe was gone.

"What's the matter, Daddy?" Hadley asked when he got back to the house, walking slowly with his hands deep in his pockets.

"Nothing, baby," he said. "Nothing you need to worry about."

He tried to give her a smile but gave up and headed inside, closing the screen door gently so, for once, it didn't slam.

All Hadley could do was watch him go.

"Heard on the radio today there's a storm coming up the Gulf."

"Hmm." Walker stared at the ice in his glass.

Gran cast a glance at her youngest son. "Hadley, hon, can you take this tray up to your mama, then wash up? Dinner will be ready in a few minutes."

"Sure, Gran."

Hadley knew when she was being gotten rid of. She took the tray up, making plenty of noise on the stairs so Gran would feel free to speak her mind.

After what little she'd heard Dr. Monroe say earlier, and her daddy's reaction to it, she was surprised to find her mother looking fit and hearty. She set the tray on the bedside table, noticing the pink in the older woman's cheeks.

"You feeling all right, Mama?" Hadley asked.

"Oh yes, baby. I'm fine as a fat kettle of fish. Just a little tired. The doctor thinks I'm overdoing it. The man doesn't understand show business at all."

Hadley smiled back at her mother. Try as she might, she couldn't see any new cause for concern. It seemed like Winnie had even put on a little weight recently.

"I'll let you rest then, but be sure and eat something or Gran will be on both our cases."

On her way down the stairs, Hadley trod lightly, stepping over the creaky third step completely, as she made her way back to the kitchen.

"Oh, Walker. Not again."

"Win doesn't get it. She pretended like Joe had told her the weather was just fine today."

"But—why don't I take stock of our supplies? You can pick up anything we might need in town tomorrow. They're saying that storm might still turn down the coast, but no point in taking chances."

She must have given herself away. Or Gran had a sixth sense about eavesdroppers. Hadley went on into the kitchen. She wouldn't learn anything else tonight. Hadley stood there and looked from her grandmother to her father, daring them to meet her eyes, but Gran had turned to the dishes in the sink.

"Sure, Mama," Walker said quietly. "Whatever you need." He rose and left the kitchen through the back door.

He never glanced in his daughter's direction.

8

"You kids sure you're going to be okay out there all alone?" Charlotte Abbott was packing sandwiches and snacks in a small basket. Her hair, the same strawberry shade as her son's, was pulled up in a messy top-knot, shining like the silver bracelets she wore around her wrists.

Hadley and Jude had never been inside the Abbott home. Hadley found herself enchanted, if a bit overwhelmed, by the sheer amount of color that surrounded them. There were vibrant paintings on the walls—walls that were themselves painted in various shades. Throw pillows of deep oranges and midnight blues nestled in the corners of the sofa.

The kitchen was bright yellow, with touches of red peeking out. There was a ceramic cookie jar in the shape of an apple and a little line of trim on the bottom of white curtains dotted with small red cherries.

There was no apparent rhyme or reason to it, and yet it all came together in a warm, welcoming mess.

Hadley thought of Gran's kitchen, with its wallpaper roses that had faded nearly away, and the butcher-block counters that were bleached and smooth from generations of wear. It was old and worn, but just as inviting, in a different way.

"Mom, stop worrying. We'll be right across the road," Cooper said.

"Telling your mother not to worry about you is an exercise in futility, son. You'd have better luck convincing the sun not to rise."

While Charlotte bustled about with an energy that was only slightly more contained than Cooper's, Dan Abbott sat reading his newspaper, a quiet presence in the midst of his family.

"If you get scared, you can always come back here. I could make some popcorn and you guys could watch movies and stay up as late as you like," Charlotte said. The idea was appealing to Hadley, who liked this place, liked these people.

"Mom, I'm almost eleven. I'm not afraid of the dark."

"You're not afraid of anything. Why do you think I worry so much?"

"We'll keep him out of trouble, Mrs. Abbott," Jude said.

A snort came from behind the newspaper.

"We'll try, anyway," Hadley added.

"And if the weather gets bad—"

"Mom, the storm's not coming in until Sunday. The radio said so."

"Okay, but—"

"Mom, we gotta go. Sam's meeting us to set up the tent."

With a sigh, Charlotte handed over the basket of food.

"Fine, then. I give up." She landed a kiss on Cooper's cheek.

"Finally," he said, but he was smiling.

"Have a good time!" she called as the three kids made their getaway.

"Sorry, my mom's weird."

"I think she's great," Hadley said, oddly defensive of a woman she hardly knew.

"It's because you're an only child," Jude told Cooper. "My mom has five. She's too busy to fuss."

Hadley was an only child. She thought of her own mother, then pushed that away.

"Race you," she said.

"Does that thing work?" Cooper asked, dropping an armful of sticks and pointing to the vintage carousel that sat next to the Dixon barn.

Dusk was settling in. The setting sun glinted off the faded grandeur of the old amusement park ride.

"Not really," Hadley said. "The lights and music come on, but it doesn't move. My dad's waiting on some parts to come in."

"Let's go see," Cooper said.

Hadley started to call him back but stopped. He couldn't hurt the thing.

"Is it okay?" Sam asked, dropping more sticks onto the pile.

"Yeah, I guess, but it's not that interesting," she said with a shrug.

"Are you kidding me?" Sam said. "Come on, Jude, let's go check it out."

Hadley trailed her friends across the field to the broken-down carousel. She watched their faces light up as they climbed on the platform to get a closer look at the animals—half horses and half an odd menagerie. There was a lion that would forever be chasing the zebra positioned in front of it. Hadley didn't share their enthusiasm, but she couldn't help but smile at their laughter as Sam put his face next to the roaring lion and imitated its fierce expression. Even Jude looked interested. But then, she'd always been fascinated by Gran's animals, as Hadley thought of them.

It had started before Hadley was born, when her dad was a kid. Coming back from Cordelia one day, on one of the lonely country roads that crisscrossed the county, they saw it.

The carousel was in sections, according to the story Hadley had heard, the horses strewn upon the ground like they'd died in battle. No one knew how it had come to be there. Hadley sometimes wondered if it had dropped from the sky.

But Alva looked at those piles of rusted gears, full of neglect, and she saw beauty peeking through. They dragged it home, section by section, Alva and her boys. And then they set to restoring it. To what end, no one could really say. Simply because Alva wanted to, Hadley supposed.

Her grandmother worked on that carousel for eight years before it was done, though she never did figure out where it had come from.

By the time Hadley came along, that first carousel was set up at the park in Whitewood. Alva had donated it to the town.

"Wasn't mine in the first place," she said. "Be a shame to keep it hidden out here in the middle of nowhere."

Since then, kids had come from all around to ride on the backs of the wooden horses Alva had so painstakingly resurrected.

Word got around. The animals came in piecemeal sometimes, shipped from across the country. Some for restoration or repair, some Alva bought and paid for, just because.

The carousel Hadley's friends were climbing around on was the third full unit her grandmother had taken in.

"You kids want to see it light up?" Gran called from the front porch. A chorus of *yes, ma'ams* greeted that, and she laughed.

It took a few minutes, but once her grandmother got the lights and the organ music going, Hadley could almost see the appeal.

Jude, Sam, and Cooper climbed on the animals, choosing favorites, changing their minds, and clowning around. Gran smiled at them with a similar sort of joy.

Cooper, especially, seemed charmed by the vintage ride. After climbing up on the back of the lion, he stood and shouted orders to the others. A pirate captain under siege. A safari king of the bush.

He's too big for this place, Hadley thought, standing to the side. *Whitewood can't hold him forever.*

The carnival music brought Hadley's dad to the door of the barn. He watched without coming any closer. Hadley waved to him, but he must not have seen her.

The sun was dropping below the horizon, the dark encroaching everywhere but the carousel. The kids were spotlighted on a darkening stage, stars of their own show.

The spectacle brought another observer, one Hadley might not have noticed if her eyes hadn't passed that way.

Eli.

He watched from a distance. No one saw him but Hadley. Even with the laughter all around her, a touch of fear snaked its way up her spine.

"Hadley, I . . . I heard my mama and daddy talking last night," Jude said, sitting cross-legged next to her friend. They were seated near the ashes of the makeshift campfire they'd roasted marshmallows on earlier. It was late. The boys were asleep in their sleeping bags inside the old tent from the Dixons' barn. When Hadley had crept out to sit under the stars, she'd thought Jude was sleeping too.

They'd pitched the tent in the corner of the field next to the woods. They could hear the river singing its song through the darkened trees. In the distance there was a soft yellow glow from the porch light Gran had left burning. The kids had played at roughing it in the wilderness, a forgotten band of child gypsies left to make their way in the world, at least for a few hours. They'd been determined to wring every last drop of freedom from the night, but each of them was aware that parents lay in all directions.

They were still young enough to be secretly comforted by that.

"Yeah?" Hadley said, waiting for Jude to continue.

"They didn't know I was there. I'd gone to bed, but I got up to get a glass of milk, and their door was open."

It occurred to Hadley how much easier life would be if parents would tell kids things instead of making them sneak around.

"They were talking about your mama."

Hadley sat up straighter.

"What did they say?"

Jude opened her mouth, but there was a noise behind them. Both girls turned to find Sam standing there.

"Sorry," he said. "I wasn't trying to listen in, I swear. I couldn't sleep. Cooper's thrashing around in there, talking in his sleep. Something about wishes and fish."

"It's okay," Jude said. "We can talk about it another time."

"No," Hadley said quickly. The wondering would drive her crazy.

"I'll just go back in the tent," Sam said, embarrassed and turning to go.

"That's dumb." Hadley was too impatient to be nice. "Just sit down. It's no secret my mama's crazy."

Sam hesitated a moment, then sat next to Jude in the damp grass.

"Tell me," Hadley said.

"I didn't really understand it all, but it sure sounded like . . . Hadley, is your mama gonna have a baby?"

Whatever Hadley thought Jude might say, that wasn't it.

"A . . . a baby?" she stammered. "No . . . I mean, how could . . . ?"

"I know you know where babies come from," Jude said. It would have been hard to not know, growing up in the country, in a farming town.

"No, I mean, yeah . . . but . . . wouldn't I know?"

Jude shrugged. "My mom'd never be able to hide that huge belly she gets, but I guess it depends on how close her time is."

Hadley thought of the fullness she'd noticed in her mother's face, the blush on her cheeks. And the way she almost always wore a cotton nightgown that floated around her frame.

With a start, Hadley realized she rarely saw her mama when she wasn't seated at her vanity or tucked into bed. She sometimes saw her wandering down to the river, but always from the distance of her bedroom, with the darkness of the night between them.

Jude and Sam were watching the emotions cross her face. There were plenty.

"There's something else, though," Jude added with a frown. "I'm not sure, but it sounded like maybe this isn't the first time."

Hadley shook her head, more confused than ever. "But . . . but then, where are the others?"

Jude looked troubled. "The thing is . . . Well, I think maybe . . . Hadley, I think they died."

"What?" Hadley's voice rose an octave. But Jude didn't take it back.

"I think they died and maybe that's what's wrong with your mama's head."

It was too much. She couldn't take it in. And Jude and Sam were looking at her, waiting. *Waiting for what?* she wondered.

Hadley shook her head. "I can't . . . That's just . . ." She trailed off.

At a loss for words, she felt like a bug running from a magnifying glass.

"You never asked what the fight was about," Sam said suddenly, breaking the silence.

Jude swung her head around, thrown off by the change of subject, but Hadley seized the lifeline with gratitude.

"I asked Cooper, but he wouldn't tell me," she said. Her voice almost sounded normal.

"He took my notebook."

There was a pause.

"That's it?" Jude said. "We figured he called your mama fat or something."

"Don't call my mom fat."

"I didn't call her fat. I just said Cooper could have called her fat."

"My mom's not fat."

"Okay. You don't have to get all twisted up about it. So your mom's not fat."

"What's so special about your notebook?" Hadley asked.

"I . . . It's private."

"Yeah, we figured that out," Jude said. "You have to tell us now. You brought it up."

Sam looked around, like he wanted to make sure no one was going to overhear.

"Spit it out," Jude said. "It can't be that bad."

With a sigh, Sam mumbled, "I write poetry."

"Poetry?" Jude asked loudly.

"Shhh," Sam said.

"Why? Who's going to hear us out here?" she said.

Hadley felt a pang of sympathy at the look of pure embarrassment on Sam's face.

"I just . . . It's private, and Coop's my best friend, but he doesn't really . . . get that."

Hadley could sympathize.

"So tell us one of your poems," Jude said.

"No."

"Come on," she badgered.

"Uh-uh. No way."

"I'll tell you a poem if you tell me one of yours."

"You don't know any poetry."

"Sure I do."

Hadley stood up. "I'm going to sleep," she said.

The pair took no notice.

"Twinkle, twinkle, little star . . . ," Jude intoned in a serious voice.

"That doesn't count . . ."

Hadley smiled as she slipped into the tent, then into her sleeping bag with the two of them still sparring.

But her smile faded as she lay there, the murmur of voices and occasional laughter floating in from the outside.

Jude's earlier words felt heavy. Had her friend handed her a clue to her mother's troubled mind?

Hadley examined it, like a piece of sea glass washed up on a beach. She turned it over, looking at it from all angles. Light played through it, casting images. But as bright and beautiful as some of those images were, filled with the laughter and promise of a baby brother or sister, this knowledge had a sharp edge.

Hadley ran her thumb, oh so gently, down that edge. She couldn't stop herself from wondering what it was about a baby that Mama needed so badly. What would another child give her that she couldn't find in her living, breathing daughter?

Hadley knew she'd best put that thought away. If she lingered over it, it was bound to cut her.

9

They slept late the next morning. The sun was well into the sky when their idyll came to an abrupt end. Eli Dixon opened the flap of the tent and stood over them, outlined by the morning sun.

"Time to go now."

His voice was enormous in the enclosed space, shattering Hadley's troubled dreams.

"Go now," he repeated, louder this time, his eyes red, his scarred face unshaven and menacing. The kids had bolted upright in their sleeping bags and huddled together, shaking in fear and shock.

"Don't come back," he told them slowly, in case they had trouble understanding.

"Never come back here."

Then he was gone.

A stunned silence filled the space he'd left behind.

"I told you it was a body!" Cooper said. Unbelievably, he was grinning.

The others gaped at him.

"Well, didn't I? You can't tell me that guy's not some sick, wacko killer. Did you see those scars?"

Hadley shook her head, irritated at Cooper's excitement.

"It was the dog," she said, climbing out of the sleeping bag. "I told you, my gran said the dog died. Eli was burying it."

She started gathering up the stuff scattered around the tent.

"But that's the perfect cover, don't you see? He could say it was the dog, then chop up a kid and bury it in the grave."

Cooper's hair stood on end, and he had a manic look in his eyes. It wasn't so different from the look that had been in Eli's.

"I don't care if it was the dog. He scares me, and I'm going home," Jude said, as she started throwing her things into her sleeping bag faster even than Hadley was.

"No, don't you see—"

"Cooper, cool it," Sam said, his voice sharp.

Surprisingly, he did.

10

Tropical storm Jolene has been officially upgraded to a hurricane. Currently classified as a category two, and still growing, she's expected to be a category four by the time she makes landfall sometime late Sunday afternoon. The storm will have possible sustained winds of 130 to 140 miles per hour and gusts that could reach even higher. Residents of Cordelia and the surrounding areas are advised to take all necessary precautions.

The mayor of Cordelia, Clemont Desmond, has this to say:

"Right now, we've issued a voluntary evacuation. She's a big one, folks. If you've got somewhere to go, I highly suggest you get there. For the knuckleheads that insist on riding it out, all I can say is, batten down the hatches. Tape and board up your windows. Secure everything that's not nailed down. Stock up your shelves with plenty of water and nonperishables.

"Expect and plan for power outages and downed trees. We'll have y'all up and humming again as soon as we can, but in the meantime emergency services will be stretched to their limits and then some.

"The Cordelia Convention Center and the high school gym are setting up cots as we speak, so if you don't feel safe where you are, come on and make yourself at home. The local churches and Red Cross are coordinating, but they've asked me to put the word out that additional volunteers are welcome at both shelters.

"We've seen storms before, and we'll see storms again, but this one promises to be one we'll remember, so please, folks, stay safe, and by God, be prepared. It's going to be a rough one."

That was Clemont Desmond, mayor of Cordelia, in a statement made this morning . . .

The voices from Gran's old kitchen radio spoke in the background as Hadley helped her grandmother in the kitchen. They'd already stocked the pantry with cans and gallon jugs of water from the Twin Pines Grocery. Two of Gran's big stockpots were simmering, one with gumbo, another with chicken and dumplings. Hadley was busy chopping green peppers and onion that stung her eyes for a third pot earmarked for chili.

"Why are we making so much food, Gran? The storm's only supposed to last three or four days. This would feed us for a month."

"Because the power's bound to be out for a while. What else are we going to do with all that meat in the freezer?" she said. "Besides, I'm going to take some of it down to the parish hall later. They're gonna have plenty of mouths to feed."

"Why are people staying at the church, Gran? Why don't they just stay in their houses like we are?"

"Believe me, girl, if we lived in one of those trailers in the river bottoms, we'd be knocking on the church door right about now."

"But we're right by the river too. What if it floods here?"

"We're on a high part of the county, Hadley. And you've seen how deep those banks are. If the Neches comes out of her banks here, it is truly the end of the world, and the rest of the town will be floating by shortly. I've never seen, or even heard, of that happening, and this house has weathered many a storm. The bottoms, though, they're on the other side of town, and they're bound to flood. They always do."

"But if it always floods, why do people live there?" Hadley asked.

"Because that's all they can afford, Hadley. Not everybody had a great-great-grandfather that built a big old sturdy farmhouse they can feel safe in."

Gran reached over and dotted flour on the end of her granddaughter's nose.

"Each of us receives different blessings to be grateful for, hon."

Hadley smiled and wiped the smudge off on her arm.

"Waaaal-ker!" Winnie's voice echoed through the house.

Alva glanced upward with a frown.

"And different burdens to bear," she added quietly.

"Daddy's still taping up the windows," Hadley said, glancing outside. The wind was already picking up a little. He'd be shutting and boarding over the shutters after that.

"I'll go up and see what she needs," Hadley said.

"You're a good girl, Hadley Dixon."

Hadley hopped off the wooden step stool but turned back to her grandmother before she left.

"Gran, can we send the gumbo to the church and keep the chicken and dumplings?" She'd never cared for the burned, seafoody flavor of gumbo.

Her grandmother sent her a smile.

"If that's what you want."

"Thanks, Gran!" she said and ran up the stairs to her mama.

She found Winnie agitated and pacing her room, her hair hanging disheveled down her back.

Hadley snuck a glance at her belly. As was typical, Winnie was wearing one of her voluminous cotton nightgowns. But now that she knew to look, she could see the way the gown didn't fall straight down anymore but came outward over her mother's expanding middle.

Why didn't they tell me? she wondered, fighting a surge of frustration. There'd be time for that later, though.

"What's wrong, Mama?" Hadley asked in the calm, soothing tone she'd learned worked best when her mother was upset.

"Walker. I need Walker," Winnie said, barely glancing at her daughter.

Hadley was reminded of the tiger she'd seen at the circus last year. The big cat had had the same desperate, searching eyes, as though if she looked hard enough, fast enough, she'd find the exit she knew was there somewhere.

"Daddy's outside, Mama. Getting ready for the storm. There's a hurricane coming."

"He put tape on my window. Said he's going to board it up."

"The storm's going to be a bad one, Mama. He's just keeping us safe."

"Don't want to be locked in here. I need to be able to get out. What if there's a fire? What if there's a fire and I can't get out?"

Hadley could feel the tension in her mother rising.

"No, Mama. There's no fire. There'll be rain pouring from the sky for days and days, and the wind's gonna howl something fierce, but no fire. I promise."

"Rain?" Winnie asked hopefully. Her pacing paused, and for the first time she seemed to see her daughter standing there.

Relieved to be getting through, Hadley painted the picture with bold strokes.

"Rain," she said. "Lots and lots of rain. More rain than you've ever seen."

"Rain," Winnie repeated, and Hadley could see the tightness in her face start to loosen.

Seizing the opportunity, she took her mother gently by the arm and led her to the bed.

"The whole world's going to be wet, Mama. Covered in rain. No fire could stand up to that."

Winnie nodded. Accepting her daughter at her word, she climbed into the bed.

When Hadley closed the bedroom door behind her a few moments later, she wondered briefly when Mama had been out in the woods. She hadn't seen or heard her come or go, so it had to have been last night or in the early hours of the morning.

There was no doubt she'd been, though. The dirt on the hem of her white gown and the bottoms of her feet was undeniable.

11

It was late in the afternoon by the time Alva and Hadley returned from Whitewood Methodist, and the day had begun to gray. The first spatters of rain fell across the windshield as they pulled up the long gravel drive.

Hadley was surprised to see the Abbotts standing on the porch. She looked around for Cooper but didn't see him anywhere. Walker was standing at the door, a towel hanging around his neck. He must have washed up after finishing the job on the windows. Hadley and her grandmother joined them on the porch.

"Said he was going fishing this morning," she heard Mr. Abbott say. "He usually fishes down by the reservoir, but no one's seen him."

"We thought maybe he'd come this way," said his wife.

When Dan Abbott spotted Hadley, his eyes drank her in, searching her face for an answer to a question she hadn't been asked. There was a barely controlled urgency in him that made her back up a step.

Walker looked at his daughter. His face was troubled.

"Hadley, have you seen your friend Cooper today?"

Hadley shook her head. A sliver of unease slid into her consciousness.

"No, Daddy."

Dan Abbott's face fell. "He should have been home hours ago. Sam hasn't seen him. He wasn't at the Monroes'. We hoped he was here."

He looked down into the upturned face of his wife. She said nothing.

"I think it's time to call the sheriff, Charlotte."

Mrs. Abbott nodded, fighting tears. Her husband tried to reassure her.

"He probably just got lost. The Sheriff's Department will help us find him."

She nodded again, quickly, like she was holding tight to that. Still, she didn't seem able to speak.

Hadley glanced across the field. The drops of rain weren't falling straight down but whipping from side to side as the wind had its way.

No one mentioned the weather.

"You can call from here," her grandmother said, motioning them inside.

The Caddo County Sheriff's Department brought all its available manpower, and as word spread through Whitewood that the Abbott boy was missing, more people arrived in raingear. Some of the volunteers were sent to search near the reservoir on the other side of town. Other men searched the woods up and down the river behind the Dixons' house.

Their wives, meanwhile, tried to keep Charlotte Abbott's spirits up. When that failed, they tried to distract her. With cups of tea and coffee, and sandwiches that were hardly touched, the women held their vigil. The lights burned, pushing back the darkness of a night that continued to fall, in spite of their combined efforts to hold it at bay.

Jude and her mother, Vivienne, arrived. Jude joined Hadley and together they watched silently from the edges.

Hours passed.

When the ladies ran out of platitudes, the sound of rain hitting the roof filled the kitchen. The fear grew larger in the empty spaces between their words. Mrs. Abbott's eyes darted to the windows and the strengthening storm beyond, where men with flickering lights shouted the name of her lost son.

Cooper looks so much like his mother, Hadley thought. They both have hair that looks burnished when the sunlight hits it. The same smile too, with a hint of a dimple in the left cheek. Mrs. Abbott, on a normal day, sitting among the other ladies of Whitewood, would be a brightly colored piece of silk in a field of white cotton. But there was no sunlight to shine through her hair, and her smile was gone that night. Her edges were starting to fray.

The night dragged on.

As the searchers trickled back in, bringing the rain and wind through the door with them, each with a silent shake of the head, the stiffness in Mrs. Abbott grew. The ladies' words of encouragement had run dry, and one by one they left quietly as their husbands returned, before the weather got any worse.

As they escaped the stifling thickness in the air that had settled around Charlotte Abbott, each of them felt a shameful sense of relief. Relief that it was her child. Her child, and not their own.

Vivienne took Jude home.

As Hurricane Jolene held them all in her tightening grip, only Gran, Hadley, and Mrs. Abbott remained. Hadley dozed in her daddy's chair. She woke, confused and disoriented, when her mother's robe brushed her face as she glided by.

Winnie had remained in her room throughout the long night. In unspoken agreement, Hadley and Gran had chosen to leave her undisturbed. What she might have heard or thought about the people coming and going from the house and the woods was, as always, a mystery.

Hadley rubbed the sleep from her eyes and watched her mother move silently into the kitchen.

"Charlotte, I don't believe you've met my daughter-in-law, Winnie," she heard her grandmother say.

Whatever Charlotte's reply may have been, Hadley couldn't hear, as she rose and moved toward them. But she'd drawn close enough to hear what Mama said next.

"You've lost your boy." It wasn't a question.

"Winnie, dear—" Gran began.

"You've lost your boy, and he's not coming back."

Hadley could see Mrs. Abbott's frozen face from her vantage point behind her mother.

"Winnie," Gran said, sharper now. "I don't think—"

"Once you lose them, they never come back," Winnie said before Gran turned her around and led her out of the room and back up the stairs.

Hadley was left alone with the terrified woman.

"I'm sorry," she said. "My mother's not . . . She's not right." Mrs. Abbott squeezed her eyes closed and hugged herself tightly. Hadley thought she was trying not to fly apart.

"She's wrong," she whispered. "My Cooper is coming back. He's coming back."

Hadley was spared trying to answer when she felt Gran's hand on her shoulder.

"Of course he is, Charlotte." Mrs. Abbott looked up quickly, searching Gran's face, looking for confirmation.

"He's coming back," she said again, louder this time. "He is. I should go home. I need to be there when he gets home. I should be there. He'll wonder where I've gone to. I have to go home." She looked around, like she was searching for something, but there was nothing there to find.

"I'll walk you over," Gran said, then leaned down and gave Hadley a quick, tight hug.

"I'll be back soon," she whispered.

Hadley could only nod. As she watched the women open the door to brave the wind and rain, she heard Mrs. Abbott say again, "He's coming back."

Hadley sat alone in the kitchen as the sun rose on a day that felt as dark as the night that had come before it.

They didn't find Cooper that night.

Jolene raged for four days, forcing all to abandon the search.

They didn't find Cooper in the days and weeks that followed, either.

With glances thrown over their shoulders, and eyes full of sympathy and regret, the people of Whitewood had little choice but to step back into their lives.

Across the road from the Dixons', a family fell apart.

12

Most people, if asked, would tell you that Cooper Abbott had surely had some sort of accident. Maybe he'd been bitten by a snake or fallen into the river and hit his head on a rock. There were as many rumors as people to spread them, and a thousand possibilities to choose from.

The one thing they all agreed on was that Jolene had been a true misfortune, carrying off any clue to finding the boy. Probably carrying off the boy himself, down the river toward the Gulf of Mexico.

No one suspected anything more sinister.

Not at first.

By Thursday night, the skies had cleared. On Friday, the cleanup began.

The Dixons' power was still out, as it was in many places across town, but Hadley didn't care. She was happy to be outside, helping to haul downed branches into a pile and picking up dropped nails while Walker took the boards off the shutters. Light slowly came back into the dim house.

It was just after lunch when the sheriff's car pulled slowly up the drive, gravel crunching under the tires all the way.

Ben Hammon was an old friend of Walker's. They'd gone to school together way back when and still met up for poker night every other Friday. But it wasn't a social call that brought Sheriff Hammon out to the Dixon house that day.

The sheriff wasn't alone. One of his deputies got out of the passenger side of the car. The deputy looked forbidding in his brown uniform and hat, his eyes scanning the trees behind their home. But he smiled and gave Hadley a wink when he caught her watching him.

"Hey, Ben. Any news on the Abbott boy?" Walker asked.

The sheriff shook his head. "Nothing yet. We've picked up the search again, but frankly, Walker, I don't expect to hear anything until we get a call from somewhere downriver."

Walker cleared his throat and motioned in her direction.

"Hadley, you remember Sheriff Hammon, don't you?"

She knew good and well the reminder was for the sheriff, so he wouldn't say anything else that meant something. *Cooper is my friend,* Hadley thought, tired of being treated like a baby.

"Actually, Walker, we'd like to speak with Hadley, if you don't mind."

Walker's eyebrows shot up.

"What's this about, Ben?"

"Dan Abbott was in to see us as soon as the weather let up," the sheriff said. "He says the kids had a run-in with your brother last weekend."

The campout. An image of Eli looming over them in the doorway of the tent filled Hadley's mind.

"Eli?" Walker asked, glancing down at Hadley, clearly confused. She hadn't told him what had happened last week, and so much had happened since.

"What's Eli got to do with anything?"

The sheriff tipped his hat back and scratched his head, not looking entirely comfortable in his own skin.

"Probably nothing, to tell you the truth. But a boy is missing, Walker, and we have to do our jobs."

All three men turned to Hadley then. Her eyes went wide.

Walker squatted down next to her.

"Hadley, honey, you don't have to be scared. You're not in any trouble. Just tell the men here what happened. Nobody can be hurt by telling the truth."

Hadley knew that wasn't true. If it were, her father wouldn't look so worried. But she couldn't see another option, so she did as he asked. She told the truth.

13

The next day, Sheriff Hammon was back, with both his deputies in tow this time. Armed with a search warrant, the deputies searched Eli's shack while the sheriff took Eli to the station for questioning.

"I'm real sorry about this, Walker," Ben said as he led Eli to the waiting car.

Alva was beside herself. Eli never left those woods. "Eli didn't do anything to that boy, Mama. It's not possible," Walker said. But to Hadley, her daddy's words rang hollow. She wondered how he could be so sure.

If she'd been present in the sterile space of the interrogation room, she still wouldn't have been convinced.

Questions were fired at Eli over and over again, as Sheriff Hammon tried to find a crack in Eli Dixon's story. But his story was too simple to have cracks.

"Where were you on Sunday, Eli?"

"Home."

"Did you see anyone?"

"No."

"Did you hear anyone?"

"No."

"Did you leave your home?"

"Yes."

"Where did you go?"

"The river. The woods."

"Did you see or hear anyone in the woods or by the river?"

"No."

"All day long, you never saw or heard anyone? Not even your family?"

"Spoke to Walker 'bout supplies in the barn."

"When was this?"

"Sunday."

"What time on Sunday?"

"Before the storm came in."

"Where did you stay during the storm? Surely not down by the river."

"Stayed in the barn. That's why I had the supplies."

"Do you know where Cooper Abbott is?"

"No."

"Have you seen Cooper Abbott, Eli?"

"Yes."

"Where?"

"In the tent."

"What about on Sunday? Did you see him then?"

"No."

"Why did you tell the kids to go and not come back?"

"Weren't safe."

"Why wasn't it safe?"

"Just weren't."

"But why?"

"Boy's gone now, ain't he? Nothing's ever safe."

In the end, there was no evidence found to indicate Eli was connected in any way to Cooper's disappearance, and Ben Hammon was forced to let him go.

Eli retreated to his small home. He was never in the company of outsiders, so he didn't hear the talk that traveled through the town like a contagious disease.

14

Dan Abbott wasn't a violent man. But when Hadley saw him walking up their drive, she ran to get her father. "Daddy," Hadley called. "It's Mr. Abbott. He looks . . . Well, you'd better come and see."

Walker glanced out the front window and took in the sight of Dan Abbott's face. He opened the door and stepped out to meet him.

Mr. Abbott never slowed, taking the steps up the porch two at a time. Then he was in Walker's face.

"Where is he? Where is the bastard?"

"Dan—"

"He knows something. He knows where my boy is."

"Dan, Eli doesn't know—"

"Then why'd they take him in? They had to have a reason!" Mr. Abbott's voice was rising.

"Where is he? God damn it, where is my son?" He was shouting now, his control clearly slipping with every word.

Walker put his hands on Mr. Abbott's arms.

"Dan, Eli didn't hurt your son."

"How do you know that? You can't know that!"

"I can. I do. No one in this world knows Eli better than I do. The sheriff questioned him because he has scars on his face. Because when something bad happens, people turn their eyes to the man who looks like a monster. But Eli's no monster. Just a man with scars."

"I just want my son back," Mr. Abbott said. "I want my son back!"

He was shouting, but his anger had broken, leaving only despair. He started to sob.

"I want my son back."

Hadley watched her father try to comfort the man. But nothing except Cooper could fill the gaping place inside of him.

Mr. Abbott let Walker walk him home, where his wife was clinging to hope while he was losing his own.

Three years later, Dan Abbott would be dead. It was a single-car accident. A bottle of Jim Beam was found shattered in the wreckage and plenty said it was no accident at all.

As for Eli, people always whispered. The whispers were fueled by the fact that Cooper's body had never been found down the river, as so many had expected. They said Eli Dixon had never been right in the head, even as a boy. He'd never fit in.

Eli himself might have been too far removed from the town to be affected by the talk, isolated in the woods, carving his trees, but Hadley wasn't. Even as the years passed and the whispers died down, with no answer to the question of what had happened to Cooper Abbott, those suspicions stayed rooted in Hadley's mind.

She didn't dwell on them. She had other things to dwell on by then, and there was nothing she could do about them anyway. But they never went away entirely.

That would've been impossible. Charlotte Abbott was just across the road, turning into a ghost in a house filled with color, where the happy sounds of a young family were only distant echoes haunting empty rooms.

15

"Something's wrong with Mama," Hadley said, shaking her father awake.

Walker sat up in the bed, bleary-eyed.

"She's calling for you. Daddy, is it the baby?"

His eyes cleared. "How did you . . . ? Never mind," he said, moving quickly toward the door.

Winnie's moans could be heard from down the hall, and when her father opened her door, Hadley hung back. Winnie's head was moving back and forth, and she was curled up in pain.

Walker hurried to her side, and she grasped his arm with both hands like a woman drowning.

"It's too soon, Walker. I can't."

"Shh," he whispered, pushing the sweat-soaked strands of hair back from her face with gentle hands.

"Hush now, Win. It's gonna be all right."

But instead of finding comfort in his words, Winnie became more agitated, groaning in pain and thrashing her arms and legs.

"You don't know that. It's not all right, Walker. It's never all right!"

She kicked the bedding awry and Hadley gasped at the blood staining Winnie's white nightgown and the sheet below.

"Hadley," her father said in a calm voice, "go wake your gran. Then I want you to run across the road and get Dr. Monroe."

She stood speechless, transfixed by the spreading crimson stain.

"Hadley!" Walker said, snapping her attention back to his face. She could see every line there pulled taut.

"Go get your gran, then fetch the doctor. Hurry now, girl."

She gave him a jerky nod. Then she ran.

Afterward, Hadley wondered if the weight of responsibility was too heavy. If it was just too much to place on the shoulders of a new life—to expect an infant to cure a woman's mental illness, to fill the massive black hole that drilled through the center of her mind. Maybe that was why he never drew a breath. He'd already suffocated under the layers of his family's need.

Her little brother came into the world silently in the night. Tiny, lovely, and dead.

The same night, under the same stars, her mother surrendered, raising a white flag to all her demons.

The doctor had gone. Walker had fallen into a restless sleep in the old wingback chair next to his wife's bed. Winnie didn't wake him, or even glance in his direction, as she floated past on bare feet.

Winnie walked out of the house to the barn, only hours after giving birth to her stillborn son. In the shadows cast by an unflinching moon, while her terrified daughter watched from her bedroom window, Winnie bathed herself in gasoline. Then she calmly lit a match and went up in flames.

From the moment she pushed her child, blue and unbreathing, from her body, until she collapsed within the fire she'd created, Winnie didn't utter a sound.

But Hadley would hear her mother's silent screams echo through the night for the rest of her life.

16

Gazing out the window of her mother's old room, Hadley watched her daughter run through the sunlight and the tall grass as she played in the field next to the old house.

She could hardly believe Kate was eleven now, looking coltish with her tanned legs and knees that were still knobby.

Hadley thanked God for her every day.

As for the long-eared puppy that was chasing Kate around with its tongue hanging out, she had her reservations.

Kate had looked reverent as she'd accepted the fuzzy bundle from Walker.

"Can I keep her?" she asked, looking up at her mom.

Hadley hesitated, put on the spot. That was surely what her father had had in mind when he'd presented his granddaughter with the silly thing without any warning. She'd shot him an irritated look.

Then Kate squealed as the puppy tried to cover each inch of her face with what seemed to be an exceptionally large tongue for such a little dog.

Hadley had sighed.

"Think of it as a welcome-home gift, sweetheart," Walker said.

"You could have just baked a cake or something," she'd told him.

But as she stood at the window and watched Kate's dark hair fly behind her, a ghost of a smile played across her face. It was a small price to pay, she supposed, to see Kate happy.

The last six weeks had been hard on both of them.

Hadley abandoned her still mostly full boxes and went to help her grandmother with lunch. She wasn't getting anything done up here anyway.

"You could have talked him out of it, you know," she said to Gran as she slipped an apron over her clothes and took up her familiar role as kitchen helper.

"Maybe," Gran said. "But why would I want to?"

"Oh, I don't know. Feeding, training, dog hair, housebreaking, chewing on shoes?"

"Honey, I'm seventy-six years old. What do I care if my shoes get chewed on?" She handed Hadley a ripe tomato. "Now slice that for sandwiches and quit your bellyaching."

"Yes, ma'am," Hadley said.

It was good to be home.

"Hadley Dixon?"

The voice echoed down the school hallway, deserted now that the first bell had rung.

"Is that really you?"

She turned to find a tall man in gray slacks and a white shirt sporting a tie covered in stylized Chihuahuas.

She tilted her head. "Sam Brooks?"

He smiled. "I heard a rumor you were back in town. You're not in trouble with Gilmore for punching someone in the nose again, are you?"

"Gilmore's still here?" she asked, looking around unconsciously, halfway expecting him to materialize behind her and demand a hall pass.

"Oh yeah. The rest of us get old, but he never does. The kids think he's probably a vampire." He lowered his voice. "The faculty too, for that matter."

"Are you . . . Do you teach here?"

"Fourth-grade reading and reluctant gym coach."

"Coach? So Coach Bagley is gone?"

He nodded. "That was a helluva scandal a few years back. He and Mrs. Huffman were caught together in the gym closet. Big, nasty mess. Divorces all around. I hear the two of them are out in Florida now, though, so all's well that ends well, I guess."

Hadley couldn't help but smile at him. He had the same easy manner he'd had as a kid, but there was something different too. A quiet confidence that said he was a man comfortable in his own shoes.

She realized suddenly how rare a thing that was.

"The real question is what brings you to our fine establishment, Ms. Dixon? Was it the smell of old socks and glue that drew you in?"

"It's Leighton now, actually."

Did she detect disappointment flashing across his eyes, or was that her imagination?

"I'm here to register my daughter, Kate. She'll start tomorrow, I hope."

"Outstanding," he said. "So you're staying, then. In Whitewood. You and your family?"

Definitely fishing. She decided to get the worst over with. He'd find out soon enough anyway.

"Kate and I've moved back home with my dad and Gran. I lost my husband two months ago. I'm a widow."

But I lost Jimmy long before I become a widow, she thought.

Sadness crossed Sam's face, and she found it oddly endearing. More so than his potential interest in her as a woman.

"I'm sorry, Hadley," he said, subdued. "Thank you," she said. "It's been hard on Kate. Do you believe in fresh starts, Sam?"

He considered her for a moment.

"I believe that life is full of tragedy. Some lives more than others. But I also believe that comfort can be found with the people who love you . . . if you're willing to let them give it."

Hadley looked away.

"Still a poet, I see," she said.

He smiled and let the mood shift.

"That's me. The kids call me Coach Shakespeare."

"Do they really?"

"No."

The laughter was unexpected, and she covered her mouth at the unfamiliar sound.

"And what about you, Hadley? Word is you're a hotshot artist in New Orleans."

"I wouldn't go that far."

She regularly sold pieces on commission in several low-key galleries in the French Quarter, but the life, not to mention the paycheck, of an artist wasn't exactly a stable one.

Especially an artist who hadn't picked up a brush in months.

"Sam, shouldn't you be teaching a class or something?" she asked.

He looked down at his watch. "Yes, actually. They're probably feeding on each other by now."

But he made no move to leave.

"It was good to see you, Hadley Dixon." She didn't correct him again.

"You too, Sam."

And to her surprise, she meant it.

17

Gran was shaking pills from an orange bottle. When she saw Hadley, she put the bottle away and washed a few down with some iced tea.

"Everything okay?" Hadley asked, taking a small plate out of the cabinet.

"Fine, fine," Gran said. "Just the perils of old age. Nothing to worry about."

Hadley laid a slice of pecan pie on the plate and sat on the barstool at the counter—old habits that slipped back on like a favorite pair of gloves.

Hadley had spent countless hours like this after her mother died.

Winnie's ashes were buried in the family cemetery on the other side of the field. The piece of land was tucked in near the trees, under an ancient willow that stood guard over old stones, letting ribbons of light through to dance on the ground below.

The baby was buried alongside Winnie, the fourth small grave in a row, marked with heart-shaped flagstones placed flat upon the earth. No names, no dates.

Hadley hadn't attended the small service. She had been unresponsive for weeks after seeing her mother die in flames and moonlight.

Eleven days after Winnie's death Gran had found her in her mother's room, sobbing into Winnie's pillow. But no matter how deep the pain sliced, her tears couldn't last forever. Tears were the easy part.

She tried, for a time, to go back to school, but she found she couldn't make it past the front porch. Her legs felt paralyzed and everything seemed muffled, like someone had wrapped cotton around the world. Or around Hadley. The only place she felt almost normal, almost real again, was with her grandmother, in this kitchen.

Walker and Alva discussed it, and finally they decided to home-school her.

Hadley could still remember the massive sense of relief she'd felt. Like she'd been dragging a bag of rocks behind her that was suddenly cut free.

"You still have to do the work, Hadley love. It's no free ride."

But she didn't mind. Not if she could stay here, in this warm, faded place with Gran. Here, where she was safe.

Hadley worked hard and got good marks, doing nothing to jeopardize her cocoon, her protection from the outside world.

Then, one day, without a word, Walker pulled out her paints and easel and set them up on the porch. She hadn't touched them since . . . before.

"Tomorrow, after you've finished your lessons, we're driving up to Cordelia. There's a man I want you to meet."

"But, Daddy—"

"No buts."

That man was Howard Cole. He was an old redneck who talked with an accent so thick it was almost comical. He was also an artist.

The first time Walker dropped her off there, she had been mute with fear. The world was muffled again.

Who knew what Mr. Cole thought of that small, pale, frightened child sitting silent in his studio?

But then he started to paint. As he painted, he talked. He talked about how to prime a canvas with gesso and lay down an undercoat. He told her why he added purples whenever he wanted black. He told her how he was using the fan brush to make trees. He kept up a constant stream of commentary in his deep Texas twang.

And slowly, the cotton had fallen away from the world.

"Any luck in Cordelia today?" Gran asked, breaking into Hadley's memories.

"Yeah, I think so. I found a printer who says he can make giclée prints for me in small batches. If it works out, I'll be able to set up a website and sell online."

Hadley rose to rinse her plate.

"In the meantime, I thought I'd look around in town, see if anyone's hiring."

Her grandmother gave her a small frown.

"Why don't you start working on something new? Didn't you say something about shipping originals to New Orleans?"

To do that, she'd have to paint. But every time she looked at a canvas, her mind went blank.

"Just something part-time. To keep me busy."

Gran looked like she wanted to say more, so Hadley quickly put her plate in the dishwasher and gave her grandmother a kiss on the cheek, then joined her dad and Kate on the front porch.

"Pull up a seat, kid," Walker told her.

"Granddad is cheating," Kate said.

"Cheating at what?" Hadley asked, taking in her daughter's flushed, dirt-smudged face and tangled hair, the stupid dog lolling at her feet.

This place was good for Kate. She hoped.

"There's no way one person can know what every candy in the world tastes like. He even guessed the divinity we brought from New Orleans."

"Oh, that game. Kate, I promise you he's not cheating. I played that game with him for years. You're not going to stump him."

"He's peeking."

"Now why would I do that?" Walker asked.

"He's guessed everything I've given him!"

"If there's one thing your grandfather is an expert on, it's candy. Sorry, babe."

"Come on, Buttercup," Kate said, and the little dog popped up. They were off and running.

"I hope she wasn't too much trouble today."

"Are you kidding? Your gran is over the moon to have you girls here. She missed you."

"What's the medication for?" she asked.

"Blood pressure."

Hadley's brow furrowed.

"The meds keep it under control, though, hon. Nothing to worry about." He patted her hand. "Your gran's gonna outlive us all."

She let it drop.

"I got Kate registered for school this morning. She starts tomorrow."

"Good. I don't think this one's cut out for homeschool," he said.

"No." Hadley smiled. "She's a different kind of kid than I was."

"Nothing wrong with that."

"I ran into Sam Brooks while I was there."

Her father's eyes zeroed in on her face, and she tried not to blush.

"Did you now?" he asked slowly, his grin spreading.

"Yes, but I don't see why you've got to look like that about it."

Kate came running up to them, breathless.

"Look, Granddad," she said. She poured something into his hand. "Look what I found."

Hadley realized what was about to happen a moment too late.

Walker, who was still grinning at her, didn't see his granddaughter's complete and utter horror when he brought his hand up and popped the contents into his mouth.

Kate gasped and slapped her own hand to her mouth.

"Dad—" But that brief, valiant hope was cut short when they heard an awful crunch. Hadley and Kate could only watch as a look of consternation crossed his face.

"Sweetie, what are these?" he asked, through a mouthful of the freshest snail east Texas had to offer. He gave one last confused crunch before he registered the look on his granddaughter's face. He rose quickly and moved to the edge of the porch, spitting onto the ground with impressive speed. But it was too late. For the snail and for his dignity.

Wiping at his tongue with the sleeve of his shirt, he looked a little green when he excused himself and hastily headed into the house.

He had to pass by his mother, who was coming to join them.

"Walker?" she asked, when she saw him licking his sleeve, but he didn't stop to explain.

"What in the world was that all about?" Gran asked.

Once Hadley recovered her voice, she looked at Kate, who was still gaping like a largemouth bass.

"I told you he wasn't peeking."

Kate choked off a hysterical laugh, then looked at her mom with big eyes.

"Oh my God, I didn't mean to . . . I just wanted to show him what I found!"

"Is someone going to tell me what's going on around here?" Alva said.

Once Hadley had painted the full picture for her grandmother, Alva looked as shocked as Kate had. At the sound of footsteps from the house, they all turned toward the front door. There stood Kate's snail-murdering grandfather, with a toothbrush hanging out of his mouth and a sheepish look on his face.

Gran burst out laughing. It was a loud, earthy bray of pure amusement. She laughed so long and so hard she had to sit down right there on the porch and wipe the tears out of her eyes.

Walker offered to take them all to the Rainbow Café for ice cream, but Hadley passed, and Gran said she'd had quite enough excitement for one day, thank you very much.

"Looks like it's you and me, Katy-did."

Hadley watched them drive off from the shade of the porch.

Movement caught her eye. There, at the edge of the trees. She squinted, covering her brow to shade her eyes from the sun.

It was Eli.

She had no idea how long he'd been standing there. Watching, the way he always had.

Without any thought or plan, she stepped off the porch and headed in his direction.

She was halfway there, cutting across the field, when he turned away and began to walk back through the trees, the shadows closing around him.

Hadley began to run.

At the edge of the woods, she peered down the path through the pines and brush.

He was there, headed for the river, in no particular hurry.

Hadley's fear of this man, this creature who'd always existed on the fringes of her world, was palpable. And this had always been his domain—his carvings on his trees by his river.

"Hey!"

He didn't stop. He didn't slow. He didn't speed up.

It's like he's a ghost, she thought. Or maybe that was her.

"Hey!" she yelled again.

Finally, he turned to face her.

Thankful, suddenly, for the thirty yards between them, she swallowed her fear.

"That little girl . . . ," she said. "That's my daughter. You stay away from her."

Eli stared at her, his expression unreadable. Hadley's heart was beating in her throat, but she didn't back down.

Then he spat in the dirt at his feet, turned his back to her, and began to walk away.

"Do you hear me? I said stay away from her!"

Eli never altered his slow, steady pace.

Hadley knew it was pointless, but her nerves hadn't settled yet and she couldn't stop herself.

"Gran, don't you think it's strange, the way Eli lives?"

Her grandmother didn't look up from her book. "Not really."

"But why does he live out in the woods all alone? Why doesn't he ever step foot in the house? He's your son. Doesn't that bother you?"

Gran sighed and set the book down. "No, Hadley, it doesn't bother me. It's what he wants. Should it bother me?"

Her grandmother's attitude when it came to Eli never changed. Hadley had stopped questioning it a long time ago. It was an unspoken rule in the Dixon house that the subject was off-limits.

"Eli's not like other people," Gran said. "And if he wants to live in the woods and be left in peace, I don't think that's asking too much. Do you?"

She practically dared her to disagree. Hadley had no choice but to accept it.

"Now, if you'll excuse me, I think I'll go lie down. I'm feeling my age today."

And with that, the subject was closed.

18

"Let's go, babe. You don't want to be late on your first day."

"I think I kind of do," Kate mumbled.

"I'm going to swing by the hardware store today and pick up some paint for my room," Hadley said.

"Oh, can I paint mine too?" Kate asked, picking up the feet she'd been dragging.

"Sure. What color do you want?"

On the drive to Whitewood Elementary, they debated the merits of various shades, but when Hadley parked the car in the lot and opened her daughter's door, Kate looked spooked again.

"Get your rear end out of this car or I'm going to paint your walls brown-and-yellow plaid."

Kate gave her a frown but climbed out of the car. Hadley walked her to the big double doors. She'd planned to walk her all the way to her first class, but Kate glanced around at the other kids heading in alone.

"Mom, I got it from here."

Hadley felt a shade of sadness at that, but she smiled at her daughter anyway.

"That's my girl. Knock 'em dead."

She resisted the urge to lean down and hug her. Instead, she watched Kate run through the doors alone.

"I love you, Katy-did," she whispered to no one.

She'd turned and was heading back to her car when she heard Sam call her name. She stopped, and he jogged over. His tie was covered in penguins wearing sunglasses.

"We've got to stop meeting like this," she said.

"Go out to dinner with me," he said, without preamble.

When she hesitated he plowed ahead. "Not on a date. It's too soon for that, I know. Just . . . Just two old friends catching up."

"Sam, I . . ."

She had no idea what to say.

"I could pick you up at seven. Or we could meet there, if that feels too date-y."

She considered him. Then she considered his tie.

"Two friends catching up?"

"Absolutely."

"Okay," she said finally and watched as he tried unsuccessfully to conceal his smile.

"I'll meet you there," she said firmly, and he nodded.

"Deal. The Voodoo Queen, tonight at seven."

They heard the first bell ring.

"I gotta go," he said. "See you tonight." He jogged off the way he'd come, and Hadley shook her head, wondering what she'd gotten herself into.

The Voodoo Queen was on the square in Whitewood. It had been there since she was young, and Hadley remembered it as a dimly lit, seedy sort of dive.

But that's not what she found when she opened the door, the bell dinging above her head.

The place was bright, clean, and surprisingly busy for a weeknight.

There was zydeco music playing over the speakers and a football game on two screens, one at either end of the bar. The waitresses were casual in jeans, black half-aprons, and T-shirts in different colors, all sporting the Voodoo Queen logo on the back.

There was beer on tap, laughter and smiles from the patrons, and, most important, the spicy aroma of Cajun food.

She spotted Sam at a booth next to the big window that looked out on the street. He waved and she made her way over, passing a waitress with a tray full of jambalaya that had her mouth watering.

"Wow," she said, slipping into the seat across from Sam. "This place has changed for the better."

"This is Jude's place now," he said.

"Really?" she said, looking around again with fresh eyes. "Of course it is," she said quietly.

"You didn't know?"

She shook her head. "Jude and I . . . drifted apart after. After Mama died."

There, she'd said it. It never got easier to say, even after all these years.

He nodded, but she saw a hint of something there, behind it.

"She tried, you know. We both did."

The weeks and months following her mother's death were still hazy in her mind. Probably always would be.

"I . . . I was never the same after that. I didn't know what to say to people. So I stayed away."

He was looking at her. Waiting to see if she would, or could, say more.

"It was a long time ago."

"Yeah," he said. "I suppose it was."

"Let's talk about you." *And not me,* she thought.

"Not much to say, really."

"Not married?"

He shook his head. "Not me. Came close once. A girl from college."

"So what happened?" she asked. "I'm sorry, you don't have to answer that if you don't want to."

Sam gave her a small smile.

"We wanted different things. I'm a small-town guy, and she was from Dallas. I took the teaching position here after graduation. She visited once and had a hard time hiding her horror. We split not long after that. Her idea."

"Sam Brooks, don't tell me you actually have a date. I might just faint dead away."

The voice came from behind Hadley, but it was unmistakable.

Sam looked up over her head. When he smiled, his eyes crinkled and his straight white teeth looked like a toothpaste commercial.

"Since you keep turning me down, I had to resort to drastic measures."

"I never once turned you down. I just said I had to bring my husband . . . along."

Jude's voice trailed off when she drew up to the table and saw who Sam's "date" was.

"Hadley," she said. "As I live and breathe."

"Hey, Jude."

"I heard a rumor, but I didn't put much stock in it. Figured you'd never come back here for good."

Hadley smiled. It was awkward, but under the awkwardness, she was happy to see the girl who'd once been her friend.

"I've moved back home. Me and my daughter."

"Daughter?" Jude said. "You have a child." It didn't sound like a question.

"Kate. She's eleven."

Jude's eyes clouded a bit.

"What about you? Any kids?"

"No, no, not me," Jude said. "Just my husband, Mateo, and I. The Voodoo Queen's our baby."

"This place is amazing, Jude."

"Thank you," she said, looking around like she was seeing it for the first time. Or seeing what it used to be. She smiled, a real smile then, one that reached all the way to her eyes.

"It is, isn't it? I'm such a badass."

"No argument there," Sam said.

"Why don't you join us?" Hadley asked.

"Oh, I don't want to cramp Sam's style. First date he's had in four damn years."

"It's not really a date," Hadley said. "Just old friends catching up. Wouldn't be the same without you."

Jude hesitated, then untied her apron, calling over her shoulder, "Can I get a round of beers over here, when you get a sec, Bill?"

"Sure thing, boss lady," the bartender said.

"Scoot that skinny white butt over, Hadley. I swear, girl, you are still the palest person I've ever seen in my life."

Hadley smiled. "We're not all lucky enough to be blessed with your beauty and charm."

"Damn right."

A drink and a big, spicy meal with two people she could honestly say she was glad to have back in her life turned out to be just what Hadley needed. And she hadn't known she'd needed anything at all.

She barely touched the beer, switching to iced tea, but it didn't matter. Before she realized it was happening, several hours had passed, and the staff was shutting the place down around them.

"We'd better get out of your hair," Hadley said. They rose to go, but Jude stopped them. "You know, if you're really looking for part-time work, I could use a hand this weekend. I have a catering job for an anniversary party, and one of my regular girls broke her ankle yesterday. Leaves me in a jam. The pay is crap, but you'd be doing me a favor."

"I should warn you—I'm a terrible waitress. I tried it in college and managed to spill enough drinks that I actually owed the restaurant money by the time they fired me."

Jude waved her off.

"It's buffet-style. We'll set up and take down and keep it full in between, but I swear on my daddy's grave not to hand you a tray of drinks."

Hadley thought it over. "Okay, yeah. If you're sure, I'd love to."

"Honey, I'm always sure. And why don't you bring Kate along? I'd love to meet her."

Jude smiled and gave her old friend a fierce hug. But for the first time since the meal began, that cloud was back in Jude's eyes.

19

"How was your date last night?" Kate asked, with just a touch of snottiness.

"I told you, it wasn't a date," Hadley said. "It was a group of old friends catching up."

Her daughter arched a brow at her from the other side of the bed they were covering with old sheets.

"If it wasn't a date, why did you mess with your hair for an hour?"

"I did not!"

"You did."

"For your information, it was practically a job interview, Miss Smarty-Pants."

"A job doing what?" There was that snottiness again.

"Helping to cater a party."

"Are you cooking?"

"No, although you don't have to sound so shocked. I can cook, you know."

"Yeah, but you don't."

"Hey, what's with you today?" Hadley asked as she opened a gallon of paint.

They were starting in Winnie's old room first, with a sea foam green that Hadley hoped would be calming. She'd taken out most of the old furniture while Kate was in school, planning to trade it out for other pieces she'd found in the attic. The room was nearly empty now.

Except for that damn bed. It was too big to move.

Kate sat down on the bed and picked at a fingernail.

"What's wrong, Kate?" Hadley asked. Abandoning the paint cans, she sat next to her daughter.

"Do you miss your old school? Are you sorry we moved here?"

"Yeah, a little, but no, I mean, I like it here. School's fine."

"Then what is it? If you tell me, I can try to help."

Kate looked sideways at her, took a deep breath, and plunged ahead.

"Are you going to get married again?"

"Oh, honey . . . Is that what you're worried about?"

"Jenny at school, her mom's been married four times, and it sounds awful. I don't want a stepdad."

"Oh, Kate, no. I'm not getting married again."

"Not ever?"

"I can't say never, no, but I'll make you a deal. I will never get married unless you say it's okay."

Kate met her eyes. "Are you serious?"

"As a heart attack."

"But what if you fall in love with a guy who doesn't like me?"

"Katy-did, I could never, and I mean ever, love a man who didn't love you too. We're a package deal, ma'am. A team."

"Really? Pinky swear?"

"Pinky swear."

"Okay," Kate said. "But it was an hour."

"It was a half hour, max, you turkey."

They made good time. Kate loved to paint as much as her mother did, and they worked well together. In a matter of hours, the room felt fresh, cleansed of any obvious reminders of Winnie. Maybe Hadley's dreams would be less troubled.

She caught her daughter in a hug. "Thanks for your help, babe. Why don't you go wash up and see if Gran needs a hand with dinner?"

"Okay, Mom."

Hadley cleared the paint away and cleaned up the mess. She had about a quarter gallon of paint left that she wanted to tuck away in case she needed to do any touch-ups later, so she dragged the stepladder to the closet and placed the can on the top shelf.

When she tried to push it back farther, though, it wouldn't budge. There was something on the shelf behind it.

Moving the can to the side, she balanced precariously on her toes, reaching up to feel around in the dark, dusty corner.

It was a box.

Barely able to reach it, she snagged the lid with one fingertip. Slowly, she slid it forward.

It was an old shoebox, tucked away and out of sight in the room of a woman long dead. A woman who'd been an enigma to Hadley in life and, in death, a wound that had never healed.

She tried to shake off the sudden sense that this box might hold some clue to her mother's life and tragic end. That was ridiculous.

It was probably an old pair of shoes.

But as she balanced atop the ladder, the box heavy in her hands, the feeling didn't go away.

She nearly blew the dust from the top of the box, but the wet paint on the walls stopped her.

"Hadley, dinner's ready," Gran called.

She started, like she'd been caught riffling through things that didn't belong to her.

She slid the box back onto the shelf, then climbed down the ladder and went to wash her hands and face, determined to put the box out of her mind.

Probably old tax bills, anyway, she thought.

20

It was late that night, after dinner. Kate was tucked into bed. The rest of the family had retired.

Hadley had showered, working out some of the kinks from a day spent moving furniture and climbing around in the attic.

She tried to lie down and read for a while. Night sounds drifted in from the window she'd left open, hoping to dispel the fresh paint smell. The window drew her out of bed. From here, on the second floor, she had a different perspective from the one she'd had as a child.

It felt elevated above the everyday realities of life. A little closer to the tops of the pines. A little closer to the stars that winked back at her.

The box sat waiting in the closet. She hadn't mentioned it to her family.

She went to retrieve it.

This is stupid. Tax bills, she thought again. *Just open it; you'll see it's nothing. Then you can sleep.*

But when Hadley lifted one edge of the lid, she let out a long, slow breath.

There were a few papers at the bottom of the box and a yellowed newspaper clipping folded some time long ago. But what held her gaze was the small bound book sitting on top and the word embossed on the red cover in gold letters. *Diary.*

Hadley shut the lid. She glanced around the room, but in spite of the coat of paint in a brand-new hue and the change of furnishings, she could still see it through the eyes of the child she'd been, once upon a time.

She could hear the country music moan and feel the auburn silk of her mother's hair as Hadley let down her curlers for her. She could taste the lemon drops Winnie kept on the vanity and see the face in the mirror smiling up at her, with that faraway look in her eyes.

Not here, Hadley thought. *I can't do this here, surrounded by my mother's ghosts.*

No, she corrected. *My mother's ghosts are in this box. These ghosts are all my own.*

She shut the door quietly behind her and made her way silently down the stairs, avoiding the creaky third step.

She turned on the porch light and sat on the old swing that had always hung there from the beam.

The box was in her lap. She took a deep, calming breath, bathing in the night around her for a moment.

Then she opened the box. She pulled the diary from its resting place, running her fingers over the single word on the cover. The spine of the small volume creaked as she opened it to the first page and the swirly, girlish writing there.

Dear Diary,
I did it! I really did it! I finally saved enough money to get the ticket. It took soooo long! Tips at the Blue Diamond aren't great, and I had to hide them from Papa when I could get away with it, but when I took out the envelope I hid in my locker at work and counted it up last week I had $48. It was enough!

Today, I told Mama I was picking up an extra shift, and I walked to the bus stop (It was 8 blocks!) and I bought my ticket.

I can't stop looking at it. Nashville, Tennessee!

Papa's going to be angry. But I'm not going to let that stop me. Not this time.

I hope Mama will understand, at least. The boys, though. I'm worried about leaving them. Especially Johnny. But I'll send for them as soon as I can. Once I'm settled in.

I can hardly believe it. I'm going to Nashville! I'm going to sing in Nashville, Tennessee, in front of anyone who will listen. I'm going to tell them tonight.

Wish me luck!

—W

Hadley sat dumbfounded at the first entry in the diary. Winnie's voice was so clear in her mind. She'd heard that kind of excitement in her mother when she'd talked about imaginary shows she was getting ready for. Shows she'd put on in the dark of the night, the wind in the trees the only applause she'd ever get.

But this. This voice was different. It was young, eager, yes, but it was coherent in a way that the woman Hadley remembered couldn't have managed for long.

"What happened to you?" Hadley asked in a whisper. "What happened that broke you so badly?"

There was no answer except the cicadas in the distance.

She turned the page.

Dear Diary,

My heart is broken. How could he? How could he do that?

And Mama! She didn't even turn from the dishes in the sink when he snatched my ticket out of my hands! Not a word!

And it's not even the ugly things he said that hurt so bad. I've heard it all before. But he laughed at me!

"Sing! Damn, girl, that's rich."

I stood up to him this time, though, even though that laughter made me want to curl up in a ball and die.

"I am, Daddy! I've bought the ticket, and you can't stop me," I said.

Why did I have the ticket in my hand? Why did I need to prove it to them? So they could see it was really real? Proof I wasn't just making up stories and big dreams?

I should have kept it hidden. Then he wouldn't have taken it from me. It was so easy.

He just reached across the table and plucked it out of my hand, like it was nothing.

All my work, all my dreams, and I didn't even see it coming. I am stupid, just like he said. A stupid little bitch with big ideas, just like her mama.

But, Mama, why didn't you help me? Why didn't you say something when he grabbed me by the hair and drug me down the hallway? When he dumped the bathroom trash onto the floor? Why didn't you help me when he flicked his lighter open and caught my bus ticket on fire and dropped it into the metal wastebasket to burn?

Why, Mama? Why?

He said I should be thanking him. Can you believe that? Thanking him. That I'd be turning tricks in a week.

I'd rather turn tricks than go back there.

And all Mama said was, "Get that mess cleaned up, girl."

Didn't she ever have dreams?

Johnny tried to help me. He's a good boy. But I couldn't do it. I just couldn't.

I ran to the back room and grabbed my bag. The bag that was supposed to go with me to Nashville, but now here we sit together on a park bench on the wrong side of the tracks.

I hate them. I hate them both. I hate this place.

I wish they were dead. I do. And I wish I had the courage to go back there and do it myself.

It was a terrible account. A young girl's dreams so carelessly crushed by her own parents. Hadley's heart ached for the pain and disillusionment so clear in Winnie's words.

But a burned bus ticket? Was that enough to send a mind over the edge?

She turned the page, but it was blank. And the page after that. She flipped through the rest of the diary. The pages were all blank.

With a frown, Hadley set the diary aside. She turned to the rest of the contents of the box.

There was a marriage license, marking Winifred Hickman's union to Walker Dixon. There was an old wedding photo, taken at the county courthouse. It was yellowed around the edges and showed a young Winnie looking beautiful and haunted, leaning into her groom's side. She looked like she was sleepwalking.

There was a photo of a boy Hadley had never seen before, aping for the camera. He looked about fourteen, with auburn hair and something familiar around the eyes. One edge of the photo was blackened, like it had been in a fire.

Finally, there was a newspaper clipping, thin and brittle with age.

Carefully, Hadley unfolded it. It was an article from the *Cordelia Sun Times*, dated from 1977, thirty-five years ago. She began to read.

APARTMENT FIRE CLAIMS EIGHT LIVES

By Jason Browne

Fire struck a small apartment complex on Cordelia's east side Sunday morning, claiming the lives of eight people and leaving an unknown number homeless. Another is in critical condition and being treated for severe burns.

Cordelia firefighters received a call in the early hours of Sunday morning of a fire at Huntington Apartments, located at 120 Southland Drive, off Blackjack Road, near the Sinclair oil refinery.

The fire is believed to have started in a second-floor unit. From there, it quickly spread throughout the complex, completely destroying the roof and central section of the building, which spanned three floors.

The building housed eighteen apartments.

"It was the screaming that woke me, and then I smelled the smoke," said Jean Stein, a 29-year-old mother of four who lived with her children on the first floor of the building.

Jean and her family safely evacuated the building, then watched, along with other residents, as the fire spread, collapsing the roof of the building.

"It's overwhelming. We've lost everything. I've no idea where we're going to go. But at least all my babies are safe. Not everybody was so lucky."

Victims of the fire include Vernon and Meredith Hickman, ages 42 and 35 respectively. Tragically, the bodies of their children, Thomas, aged 12, Marcus, aged 9, Willis, aged 7, and Nathaniel, who was 3 years old, were recovered at the scene, additional victims of the devastating blaze.

The Hickman family lived in the unit where the fire is believed to have originated.

The Hickmans also have two elder children. John Hickman, aged 15, is currently in critical condition and being treated at St. Catherine's Hospital in Cordelia.

Winifred Hickman, 17, was not in residence at the time of the fire.

"That poor, sweet girl," said Jean Stein. "Her whole family dead, and the brother not expected to make it through the day. Can't imagine what that'd do to a person."

Andrew and Martha Leatham, an elderly couple who lived in the apartment unit directly
above the Hickmans, also perished in the fire.

Hadley's eyes were wide, her thoughts pulled in a dozen directions.
She looked up to find Gran standing by the screen door, sadness in
every line of her face. Hadley didn't know how long she'd been standing there.

"Did she do it?" Hadley asked. "Did she start the fire?"

Her grandmother's face was troubled. She looked as if there were
a great many things she'd like to say. But she only shook her head and
sighed. "Your guess is as good as mine."

"The brother? Did he live?"

"No, he died the next day. Winnie was with him, but from what I
understand, he never regained consciousness."

"Her whole family . . . gone," Hadley whispered. The old swing
creaked when Alva took a seat next to her. "Even if it was just a . . . a
freak accident, that's . . . it's unimaginable."

Gran said nothing, staring off into the darkness.

"And if it was more . . . ," Hadley said. "If she somehow caused the
death of her entire family, and then some . . ." Hadley tried to wrap her
head around the massive shackles of guilt her mother would have been
dragging behind her.

"Your dad lived in that apartment complex. He'd taken a job with
a contractor—wanted to learn to build things. He stopped Winnie
from running into the building. Saw her mind slip away that night.
She was never the same. Had to be institutionalized. She only learned
to function close to normal again after she managed to block out her
memories of having a family at all. That story about being an orphan,

the one you've heard all your life? That was something she made up in her own head. I guess it helped her deal with living life, day after day."

Gran stroked Hadley's hair and her voice was gentle, but it couldn't ease the effect of her words.

"There were cracks, even from the beginning. Winnie's obsession with having a baby boy? She always insisted she'd name her son John. Four little graves. We didn't tell you at the time. At first you were too young to understand, and after that . . . Well, secrets can be contagious. We didn't put names on the stones. Winnie wouldn't let us. Couldn't bear to see the name John carved into a headstone, even if she couldn't admit to herself why. And the loss of each one took a little more from her. Until, finally, she had nothing left to give."

"But Daddy? He knew . . ."

"Oh yes. Knew all along. He visited her every day in the hospital for months afterward. It seemed to help her cope while her mind built up its walls again, as poorly constructed as they turned out to be. She leaned on him, like she'd do for the rest of their time together. She felt safe with Walker. For his part, I believe he truly loved her. He must have." Gran shook her head in bewilderment. "I've often wondered why he was so drawn to Winnie. I asked him once whatever possessed him to marry a woman he knew was so damaged."

"What did he say?"

"He told me, 'We're all damaged, Mama. It just shows more on some of us.'"

21

Mr. and Mrs. Kenneth Hart celebrated their fiftieth wedding anniversary surrounded by friends and family.

Tables were set up in their backyard. Lights, strung from tree to tree, glimmered off ripples in the pool. Tiki torches cast a glow from the edges, pushing the night back.

Grandkids and great-grandkids alike ran in packs through the legs of the crowd, attending to their own agendas. Laughter rode on the breeze, carried off in every direction.

And Jude Monroe Castillo provided the food. With a little help from her friend.

Hadley recognized a few of the faces—kids she'd gone to school with, grown now, with kids of their own. She chatted with everyone, saying words that meant little. All the while, she could feel her roots settling in, grabbing hold.

Hadley kept an eye out for Kate, who'd joined one of the wandering bands of children. She scanned the crowd, looking for her daughter's dark ponytail. Her eyes stopped on Sam, standing with a group of men. Hadley was too far away to hear the joke, but she caught herself smiling when Sam laughed at the punch line.

With a mental shake, she forced her eyes to move on. They settled on a blond woman, about her age, in a blue dress.

She might have kept going, scanning the rest of the crowd, but the woman's lips were moving, in spite of the fact that no one was with her.

One too many, Hadley guessed.

The woman was making her way around the pool toward the group of men, engrossed in her one-sided conversation.

Sam never saw her coming. When the woman crashed into him from behind, he spilled his drink on himself.

With his arms lifted and dripping beer, he turned, but when he did, the woman latched onto him. Hadley could hear her hysterical giggle carry across the pool.

Sam stepped back, trying to disentangle himself from the woman's grasp, but she was a clinger. Saying something to the men behind him, he handed over his drink, then led the woman to a nearby chaise. Blonde-blue-dress fell into it clumsily, then her laughter inexplicably turned to sobs.

Sam looked around for help, clearly out of his element. But the party was loud, crowded. No one appeared interested in claiming the stray woman.

When he turned back to his charge, it was clear she'd fallen asleep, her arms and legs at indelicate angles. A marionette without strings.

Sam considered the woman for a moment. When he turned and walked away, Hadley thought he was headed back to his friends, but he passed them without a glance. She saw him look around. He seemed to be searching for something, then she saw him home in on the pool house. The little building was tucked off in a corner, dark except for the dim, flickering light from the torches.

He headed in that direction, his stride full of purpose.

Intrigued, she watched as he went inside. If he'd asked her, she could have warned him he was about to interrupt a couple who were likely to be doing naked things.

She'd seen them sneak into the darkened structure ten minutes before.

Hadley waited for it. It didn't take long. Her mouth twitched when she heard a woman's outraged scream, followed by her partner's muffled shouting.

No one noticed. No one except Hadley.

When Sam emerged from the pool house a few moments later, looking ruffled and out of sorts, Hadley silently cheered him on. She cursed the shadows that kept her from making out what he was carrying. She hoped it had been worth it.

By now, she was invested in the little drama. She watched as he shook off his embarrassment, then strode back across the patio toward the drunken woman he'd left on the chaise.

He knelt beside her, then put a hand behind her head, which had been cocked at an uncomfortable-looking angle. For one shocked moment, Hadley thought he meant to plant a kiss on the unconscious woman's lips.

But no, she saw, relieved. Instead, he placed his hard-won prize from the pool house under her and carefully laid the woman's head to rest on it.

Sam stood and surveyed his handiwork. Not happy with the result, he leaned back down and maneuvered her arms and legs into a less awkward position. With one last gesture of kindness, he gingerly moved the hem of her skirt so that she wasn't displaying so much of her charm.

When Sam moved away, Hadley couldn't hold back her laughter.

Blonde-blue-dress's head was now resting on the ring of a child's pool floaty. It was bright yellow and had the head of a duck, its expression as blank as that of the woman it was now in charge of watching over.

Hadley's laughter somehow reached Sam through the stew of other sounds. He turned, searching her out. When their eyes met he gave a small bow, with a little flourish of his hand.

"Earth to Hadley," Jude said. She followed Hadley's line of sight. "That's a good man, right there."

Hadley snapped her attention back to the pan of étouffée.

"Lots of good men out there," Hadley said.

"Hmm. Not so many as you'd think."

A little while later, Sam materialized over her shoulder.

"Take a walk with me."

"I'm working."

"I know the boss."

"Take a walk yourself."

"Jude, can I steal your employee?"

"No problem, but cleanup's in ten, and you're helping," Jude said.

"Yes, ma'am."

He linked his arm in Hadley's. She threw Jude a dirty look over her shoulder, but the other woman only said, "Don't do anything I wouldn't do."

Together, she and Sam walked away from the lights and the noise.

When she gently took her arm back, he didn't seem to mind. The silence was almost comfortable.

"My husband talked all the time."

Hadley could have kicked herself. Sam said nothing.

"We weren't doing well. I'd filed for divorce three days before he died."

The moon reflected off the still waters of a pond not far ahead. She walked that direction.

Scooping up some pebbles at her feet, she tossed one in, just to watch the moonlight waver on the water.

Sam squatted next to her and found some pebbles of his own.

"It was an accident. He worked on an offshore oil rig in the Gulf. Kate doesn't know. About the split."

Sam shot for the moon too. Ripples and waves.

"And I can't stop myself from being mad at him. He's dead, and I wish he wasn't. I wish he wasn't so I could scream at him and throw things and demand to know why. Why wasn't I enough?"

She was glad he couldn't see her tears in the dark.

True to his word, Sam helped them clear what was left of the food away, and Kate helped as well.

Hadley put on a good face, but she was on edge, in spite of the teasing around her.

She had to stop and lean her hand on the table as she was scraping out the bottom of a pan.

"Kate, honey, why don't you help Sam carry some of this stuff back to my truck," Jude said.

"Okay."

Hadley felt a hand on her shoulder.

"You okay?" Jude asked.

Hadley tried to say yes, she was fine, but she couldn't. She leaned over the trash can and vomited instead.

"I'm sorry. The smell . . . ," she said, wiping her mouth on the back of her hand.

"Here, drink this."

The water was cold on her throat. When she'd recovered some, she found Jude looking at her, not unkindly.

"How far along are you?"

Hadley wanted to hide, but she knew it wouldn't make any difference.

"Two months, seventeen days," she said on a sigh.

A last-ditch, desperate attempt to fix things, which had only left her more empty.

Jude's voice was low. "I . . . I don't have some cache of sage wisdom to pull from, but Hadley . . . I'm here. If you need anything, I'll be here."

Hadley let out a harsh laugh. "Yeah?"

She was as shocked as Jude. She knew she should stop.

"Those are easy words to say."

It was too late to take it back.

Jude recoiled like she'd been struck. Hadley opened her mouth to say . . . what?

Sick at herself, she turned away instead. Her stomach protested, but she fought it down.

She could still see the hurt in Jude's eyes.

22

Hadley drifted in that odd place that borders sleep and wakefulness. She didn't know how much time had passed when she woke with a gasp. She thought she might have been dreaming of her mother. She tried to clear her head of the broken images, but she could almost swear she'd seen light flickering from her window. She rose from the bed and moved to the window and the view Winnie had lived with during her good days and her bad. She needed to see for herself.

It was a clear night, the moon still shining. It would have been impossible to miss the figure of her uncle walking away from the house, headed toward the river. What was he doing sneaking around in the dead of the night? Maybe it was the lingering effects of the dream. Maybe the darkness made it harder to ignore the fears she pushed down during the day, telling herself they were silly and irrational. For whatever reason, all the suspicions Hadley had tried to put aside over the years, each and every one of them, came roaring back to life. They filled her ears with a buzzing panic. She thought of Cooper. Her family's assurances that Eli was incapable of harming a child suddenly rang false and did nothing to calm her. The fact that she'd clearly seen that Eli was alone meant nothing either. One thought rang out, clear and true, above the panic.

Kate. She had to see Kate. She needed to see her daughter. Safe in bed. Touch her face, her hair, her warm skin. Safe. In her bed. Safe.

Hadley bolted out of the room and flew down the stairs, silent on bare feet in spite of the screaming in her head.

When she threw open Kate's door and her eyes landed on her daughter's sleeping form, only then did she manage to draw a breath.

She had another moment of paralyzing terror as she moved quietly into the room, sure that Kate would be cold when she reached her.

She wasn't. She was just where she should have been, safe, sound, and warm. The puppy raised its head and gave one, two thumps of its tail from the foot of the bed.

Hadley collapsed on the floor with her back against the mattress, listening to her daughter breathe. She buried her head in her hands and sobbed silent, irrational tears of relief.

Kate was safe.

When the tears tapered off and the adrenaline-fueled hysteria left her, she was exhausted and empty. She couldn't go back to her own room. Not tonight.

Instead, she crawled into the bed next to Kate, pulling her daughter tightly against her. She stroked Kate's hair and sent up a silent prayer that she'd always be able to keep her safe. Always.

As the sun broke the endless deep of the night, Hadley slipped into sleep herself, her arms still around her sleeping child.

Hadley woke up late the next day. It was Sunday. The sounds of normalcy came from the kitchen. Daylight streamed through the windows, soothing her, allowing her to layer real life on top of her nighttime fears. Kate was gone, probably off with her silly dog somewhere.

Hadley joined Gran in the kitchen, drawn by the scents of coffee and bacon.

"You're getting a pretty late start today," her grandmother said.

"Where is everybody?" Hadley asked with a yawn.

"Well, I'm not sure where your dad is, he was gone when I woke up. And my lovely great-granddaughter was out of the house early. She had a book, an apple, and her pup. What else could a girl want?"

That meant they might not see Kate until dinnertime. Hadley poured herself a cup of coffee. She should pick up library cards for them both this week.

"As for me, I'm headed into town to do some grocery shopping if you'd like to join me."

"I think I'll pass today, if you don't mind, Gran. I'm going to take a long, hot shower and work some of these kinks out. I ended up sleeping next to Kate last night, and a twin bed isn't meant for two."

"She mentioned that this morning. Said she was impressed with your supermom mind-reading powers."

Hadley tilted her head.

"Because of the bad dreams."

Hadley turned slowly back around to face her grandmother.

"Bad dreams?" Hadley asked, forcing herself to keep a normal tone in her voice.

"That's what she said. Something about how she thought there was a man sitting on the side of her bed, whispering things to her and stroking her arm."

A cold trickle made its way down Hadley's spine.

"Said she had no idea how you'd known from all the way on the second floor that she'd been having nightmares, but she was glad you'd joined her, all the same, even if she was eleven now and much too old for that."

Gran continued to talk. Hadley may have managed to respond, but she didn't remember a single word that passed. Within a few minutes, her grandmother was gone, off to run her errands. Hadley found herself alone in the house with only her thoughts for company.

She dropped into a chair at the kitchen table. She told herself to calm down. That it was nothing. Bad dreams. That was all. Hadn't she suffered the same? But she was fighting a losing battle. With every moment that passed, she was pulled deeper into the panic of the night before. Before long, she was on the verge of full-blown terror.

She tried to rein it in, to think rationally. What was going on? Had Eli been in Kate's room? When she took the sight of her uncle retreating from the farmhouse and set it down next to Kate's comments, the conclusion was staring her in the face.

He must have been. And there wasn't a reason on earth that could make that okay.

Hadley thought of Cooper, gone without a trace, like the world had swallowed him whole. She thought of her extreme fear of Eli as a child; she thought of all the whispers and the suspicions she'd put on a dusty shelf and filed away. She'd had no proof. She'd had no choice. But right now, proof didn't matter. Those suspicions were stirring, stretching their limbs and shaking off the dust of the past. And this time, they weren't inclined to be pushed back into the shadows.

What had she done, bringing Kate here? How could she have been so naive, so irresponsible, as to put her child directly in the path of such a man?

Her father might defend Eli. Her grandmother might protect him, but that was expected, wasn't it? Eli was a brother, a son, regardless of how strange and perverse his ways.

But Kate was her responsibility. Protecting her child wasn't a choice, it was an imperative branded on her from the moment Kate had taken her first breath. There was no part of her that would stand by and allow her child to be harmed. It was Hadley's job to keep that from happening, the only job that had ever mattered.

These elemental truths scraped away at her surface until she was stripped of any sense of civility or right and wrong. She had no sense of compromise or compassion. No sense of humanity. She felt feral.

Her breathing was heavy. Her skin tingled and her nostrils flared. Base instinct flooded her senses. In a matter of moments, the person she'd always believed herself to be was gone. In her place was a cornered animal whose only directive was to protect her young, at any cost.

Through the firestorm raging in her body and mind, one goal surfaced and sharpened in the heat. Protect her daughter.

Everything else subsided to a dull roar.

She would protect her daughter. She would keep Kate safe.

Hadley rose and moved with deliberate steps to her father's office. She found the Winchester .308 he kept high on a rack on the wall. There were other guns there, shotguns and handguns, a Mauser from her grandfather's time in Korea, but her eyes slid over them. The rifle was what she wanted.

The shells for the Winchester, along with the other ammunition, were kept in her father's desk drawer, like they'd always been. Hadley had never been much of a hunter, but Walker had insisted she learn to be comfortable around guns when she was a child. No one in the Dixon family hunted for sport, but guns were a part of life when you lived in the country.

Hadley loaded the rifle, feeling the cold heft of the weapon in her hand. Her course decided, she had no second thoughts. She knew if she walked this road, there'd be no turning back.

The sound of the screen door slamming broke the silence of the house, which had been holding its breath, waiting to stand witness to her next move.

Gran was back. She must have forgotten something. Hadley followed the sound of her grandmother's voice to the kitchen and saw she wasn't alone. Jude was seated with her back to the doorway, chatting with her grandmother.

"Hadley said she was going to take a shower, dear, but she'll be out soon. I'm so happy you two have reconnected. We've missed you around here."

The scene was pleasant. Hadley drank in the tranquility for its own sake, knowing she was about to blow it all to hell.

Gran looked up and spotted Hadley. Whatever thought she'd been sharing trailed off mid-sentence. Jude turned to see what had caught her attention. They both gaped at Hadley, still in her pale-yellow nightgown, the hunting rifle propped against her shoulder, pointing at the ceiling.

"Gran," Hadley said. "I'm going to find Eli. I saw him last night, leaving the house. He was in Kate's room." Her voice was matter-of-fact.

"I'm going to find him and ask him what he was doing in my daughter's bedroom while she was sleeping. I doubt he'll tell me the truth. And regardless of what he says, the likelihood is high that I'm going to kill him after that."

Alva's eyes locked on the rifle.

"I'm sorry, Gran. But as much as I love you, I will not allow anyone to threaten my daughter." There was no fear in Hadley's voice. When she turned to go, walking calmly toward the front door, her grandmother found her voice and ran after her.

"Hadley, Hadley, wait!" she called. Hadley didn't slow. Gran caught up with her in the entryway and moved to stand in front of her, holding her shoulders and looking her in the eye.

"Hadley, you can't do this. You don't understand." The rifle was between them, cold and silent.

Hadley looked at her grandmother. Her voice was gentle when she spoke. "There's nothing to understand. Eli is a monster. He always has been. You remember Cooper Abbott, don't you?" Gran flinched. Hadley might as well have slapped her.

"You can't protect him anymore. I'm going to stop him before he does more than give Kate nightmares." She moved around her grandmother, heading for the door and from there to the riverbank.

Gran didn't try to follow this time. Instead she called to Hadley's back, "Hadley, you need to hear what I have to say!"

Hadley opened the front door and stepped onto the porch.

"I'll call the sheriff," Gran called, her voice edged with desperation.

Hadley didn't turn around when she said, "Gran, you go ahead and call, but they won't make it here in time to stop me."

"Hadley, please! Stop and listen to me, I'm begging you!"

"There's nothing left to say," Hadley called back. She'd reached the bottom of the steps.

"Hadley!" Jude called from the doorway. Hadley had forgotten she was there.

"Hadley, you need to listen to your grandmother." Hadley didn't slow.

"Eli didn't kill Cooper!" Jude's voice rang out.

This time, Hadley stopped in her tracks. She slowly turned to her friend, as did Gran.

"How do you know that?" Hadley asked.

"Because Eli told me so. He also told me who did." It was Hadley's turn to stare.

"There is so much . . . so much you don't know. I almost envy you that," Jude said quietly. Then the strength came back into her voice. "But if you expect to learn any more, I suggest you come back in this house, put that gun away, put on some clothes, for God's sake, and listen to what people might have to say. You know, like a sane person would do."

23

"I'm sitting here, trying to figure out where to start," Gran said. She didn't want to look at Hadley, didn't want to see those emotions in her granddaughter, grown to a woman now and weighed down with the fears of a mother.

The three women were gathered at the kitchen table. Hadley looked tense, waiting.

"My daddy never liked Silas," Gran said finally, gazing in Hadley's direction without really seeing her. The past she'd tried so hard to keep buried was calling to her, pulling her back in.

"Even before . . . That should have been a clue. But I was too young, too dumb to listen. Too much in love." Her mouth twisted at the word.

"He was fresh off the boat, back from Korea, when we met, his pockets filled with stories of his own bravery. I knew I'd met my future. And I was right. But the rest was smoke and mirrors. Parlor tricks.

"Mama and Daddy gave us this place, you know. They inherited it from Mama's side, and I was their only child. The only one who lived, anyway."

Hazy images of a towheaded boy flitted across Alva's mind, faded memories of a brother who'd died too soon, but that wasn't the story she was here to tell, so she put it away.

"They put the deed in my name. Only my name. Another clue, one I didn't want to look too closely at. Silas noticed, though. He didn't say anything about it, not then. And for a while, things were all right.

"He might have been a little work-shy, even then, but I made excuses. Rice farming wasn't easy, and he liked to knock a few back. But a man's entitled, I told myself. Now and again.

"I let it go. And then, in the spring of our first year here, he lost his leg. An accident with the combine. After that, it all changed . . .

"The next year was nothing but a string of broken things."

1954

Silas pushed his plate across the table.

"Alva, didn't your mother teach you how to cook?"

Her eyes widened, and she looked down at the roast and vegetables on her plate. She thought they'd come out fine. Good, even. But Silas had limped in from the barn stinking of booze and looking for a fight.

"Yes, she did, Silas. I'm sorry you didn't like it." The words might have been apologetic, but the tone was sharper than she meant it to be. She rose and took the plates from the table, setting them in the sink with a clatter. It was all the excuse he needed.

He pushed his chair back and stood so quickly it tipped over behind him. When Alva turned from the sink at the sound, she found he'd already made his way to her. His eyes were dark when he grabbed her by the arm and pulled her into the dining room.

"Silas, you're hurting me," she said, hating the fear in her voice. His fingers dug in harder.

He tossed her to the floor. Her hair fell over her face, hiding the tears that were starting to flow. "Look at me," he demanded.

But she couldn't. All she saw when she looked at Silas was her own stupidity. She couldn't face it. She shook her head and kept her face buried in her hands.

She jumped when the first piece of her grandmother's china crashed to the floor next to her head. She looked up at him in shock then. But he wasn't done.

With cold precision, he chose another piece. A sugar bowl. This time his aim was better. Alva barely had time to cover her head before it hit her. She cried out in pain.

"Silas, stop!" she sobbed. "Please, Silas, I'm sorry, I'm sorry!"

But he didn't stop. Instead, he picked up a soup bowl. It bounced off Alva's hip, then broke on the floor.

She could only cry and try to protect herself as best she could while he broke it all. Not some of it, but each and every piece, one by one.

Afterward, Alva silently picked up each shard, numb with shock and pain. She could barely hear the self-recriminations. They were drowned out by the sound of dishes shattering that wouldn't leave her head. All because she'd served a dinner that didn't please him.

But the power he had over her seemed to please him fine. That much was clear from the satisfied smile on his lips as he drank in every flinch Alva gave him.

By the year's end, Silas had broken Alva's dreams into so many tiny pieces that they were dust, abandoned to blow away on the breeze. There was no trace they'd ever lived.

The only thing Silas couldn't manage to break was the promise he'd never bothered to make. The promise that Alva had foolishly inserted between the lines, all on her own. The promise of a happily ever after.

Eli's birth was a flood on parched earth. Alva found, to her surprise, that her husband hadn't managed to cauterize her ability to connect on a basic level with another human being, in spite of his single-minded attempts.

Alva named him for her grandfather. Yes, Eli was a child conceived in rape. There would have been no child otherwise. Alva had long since lost any traces of desire for her husband and refused to willingly submit, but that rarely stopped him.

And yes, she was terrified at the prospect of raising a child in the misery their house had become. No baby had any business sharing a roof with Silas Dixon. Or sharing his blood, for that matter.

But when she held her son for the first time, running the back of her finger across his tiny cheek, she clung to the perfect hope that only a new mother could understand.

Eli gave her a gift. He gave her humanity back to her. Now she had a reason to wake, a reason to love, a reason to care if she lived or died.

It was a terrible thing.

24

In many ways, the time before Eli was easier. Alva had given up, expecting nothing more than what Silas served up. After Eli, she learned about real fear. Walker came along two years later.

There were times that were good. Those times would shine through the bad like stars in the sky. Silas was prone to go on benders, drowning himself in bourbon and self-pity. He'd disappear to God knows where for days at a time. Once, he was gone almost a week.

Alva and the boys packed as much laughter and light into those hours as humanly possible. They could breathe.

Alva also managed the farm, struggling to make ends meet. She'd learned after the first season that Silas had no interest in putting work into the place that had stolen his leg. A place he knew wasn't his. So Alva hired workers when she needed them. She managed to get by. Silas's contribution was to sit out in the barn and drink the liquor the rice crop provided.

Alva didn't mind spending that money. It was a payoff, a bribe. She came to feel like she and the bourbon were allies. They both knew if he drank enough of it, he'd pass out somewhere and leave them be. And there were the boys. Her sweet boys. Alva tried to protect them from Silas. She stepped in front of his fists countless times, redirecting his anger onto her. She stupidly hoped it would be enough. But it was never enough. A hundred, a thousand beatings couldn't make up for the ones Alva wasn't able to stop. He went after the boys again and again. It became a game. He seemed to understand instinctively that to inflict the highest degree of pain on a person, you go after what they love most in the world. Alva left him once. Just the once. Silas had beaten her so badly she'd passed out. When she came to she was filled with the most intense shame she'd ever known. While Alva had lain there, useless to the world, Silas had turned his fists on Eli. She didn't know how long he had beaten him, or if he had cried out for her or begged his father to stop. When it was over, Eli crawled to where his mother lay on the kitchen floor and curled up next to her like a kitten. She barely recognized him under the pulp of bruises and swollen flesh.

Alva had no idea how long he had lain there, wondering if she would wake up or not. He was six years old.

Alva cradled Eli to her. Her arms ached from his weight and the beating she'd taken, but she couldn't put him down. She carried him, slack against her, while she searched the house for Walker. When she found him, he was on the floor of Alva's closet, curled beneath a pile of clothes he'd pulled from the hangers.

He screamed when Alva opened the door. He thought monsters had come for him. Or his father. It was the same difference.

Silas wasn't in the house. Alva didn't know where he'd gone. Maybe into town, maybe pulling one of his disappearing acts. Or maybe into the barn to drink and oil the Mauser he'd stolen off a dead soldier in Korea. She didn't dare look for him.

It was the loneliest hour of the night when Alva packed the boys and herself into the old farm truck, the three of them silent and scared. It was eighty miles or so to her parents' place, through Cordelia and into the countryside beyond. She had no idea what she planned to say, once they made it there. She only knew they needed a haven, and her father would provide it. He had to.

The three of them barely spoke on the long drive. Even Walker, who normally had plenty to say. When she did speak, she whispered to the boys, over and over again, "It's going to be okay, everything's going to be okay." She was trying to convince herself as much as them. But she was wrong.

When Alva rounded the turn to the Shepherd farm, her stomach flipped. She went pale beneath the bruises that had deepened in color during the drive. Any hope she'd had of reaching safety puffed away like so much smoke.

Silas was waiting for them at the turnoff. The Ford sedan he'd bought just after the war had more to give than the truck she drove. He must have had the pedal down to go around Cordelia by another, longer route, then gotten in front of them along Route 10. He'd been in the barn after all and heard the truck fire up. He'd known right where she'd run.

Silas could have killed them all earlier that day. Now that Alva had scraped up her courage and dared to leave him, would he finish the job?

She trembled as her husband moved toward the driver's side of the truck. He looked like a man without a worry in sight. He'd won. He knew it and she knew it. She also knew he was going to enjoy driving that point home.

Alva could hear the gravel make way below his boots, each step highlighting the limp he carried along with the prosthetic leg.

Crunch. Slide.

The sound was magnified in the suffocating silence of the night. For Alva, the world grew small. All of her focus was on those boots bringing the devil to her door.

Crunch. Slide. Crunch. Slide.

Eight. It took eight footsteps.

The truck door creaked in protest under Silas's hand, but that was the only resistance he'd see that night. Alva was frozen in place, her hands still on the wheel. Silas smiled and reached into the cab of the truck, gently combing Alva's hair over her shoulder, exposing her racing pulse. His fingers worked their way through her hair, like a lover's would. It heightened her terror. When his hand fisted in her hair, holding her head painfully in place, it was almost a relief.

"Why, Alva. What a surprise, running into you here." Silas didn't bother to lower his voice so the boys didn't hear his words. Why should he? They had no illusions about their father, even young as they were.

"This is quite the happy coincidence. You see, I've just come from your folks' place." Silas reached over with his free hand and gripped Alva's chin, turning her face to his own. Her eyes were unfocused, staring into her own personal abyss, but she heard every word.

"They're so peaceful when they're sleeping. So vulnerable. Why, if a man were bent on harm, there are so many choices it might be hard to pick just one. A knife could slice Margaret's faded old flesh right off her bones before she ever woke up."

Silas laughed.

"Now wouldn't that be a sight. And let's not forget dear old William. Maybe a baseball bat . . . Swing for the fences, right? Batter up. And if the first hit didn't do it for him, well, that's nothing to worry about. There's always the next . . . and the next. You know what they say, don't you?"

Silas's grip on her hair never weakened as he caressed her cheek with the thumb of the other hand.

"No?"

The hand holding her chin slid down, inch by inch, until his powerful fingers found her neck, exposed and tender.

"They say practice makes perfect." His grip tightened to the point of pain, then loosened again to caress her throat.

"That's assuming a man was bent on harm. So let me suggest, Alva dear, that you take these boys of mine on home and tuck them safely into their own little beds where they belong.

"After all, we'd hate for anything bad to happen now, wouldn't we?"

And like that, his hands were gone. She heard the *crunch, slide* of his boots moving away. They took with them her last hope.

25

It was Alva's birthday. She was thirty-six years old, and the weather held the promise of a cool, clear day. Fifty birthdays had come and gone in this house since she'd married Silas, if she included her own along with her sons'. That number had lodged itself in her head when she woke with the sun shining through her curtains and Silas two days gone on a bender. It was an astounding number.

Fifty. Fifty separate days, if she included the births of each of the boys. Fifty days that should have been a celebration of life and love and happiness that were anything but. There were only a few of those fifty marked by Silas's absence. She could count them on one hand, with fingers left over.

Walker's fourth birthday. The day she'd turned twenty-nine. Eli's third and eleventh birthdays. Those were cherished memories. On Eli's third, she'd baked a chocolate cake, nervous that Silas would return any minute. So nervous that after the cake was baked, she didn't give it time to cool properly before she frosted it, then called Eli into the kitchen.

The two of them sat in the middle of the floor, while she held him in her lap and sang "Happy Birthday" into his ear, her voice barely above a whisper. He beamed at her and blew out his candles. Not bothering with plates, they ate warm cake, with melting chocolate running over their fingers right there on the floor. The taste of that cake crossing her lips, together with her son's smile, was the most delicious sweetness.

Eli was sixteen now, nearly a grown man. Some days, Alva clung to that like a lifeline, knowing that soon Eli would leave this carnival freak show. At sixteen, and a big lad, he could make his way in the world, even if he came off to many as slow.

His teachers despaired of him. Most of them thought he didn't belong in the public school. But Eli could read fine, and he was competent enough at his written work. The problems came when he had to interact with others, in particular others with authority. He'd hang his head, either not answering their questions at all or mumbling a response so low and garbled no one could make it out.

Eventually, as Walker got older, the school allowed Eli to accompany his younger brother in Walker's classes. Eli ended up behind in his studies, but it was a fair compromise. Eli wasn't wound so tightly when Walker was in the room. He still chose not to speak unless it was necessary, but the teachers and other students grew used to his presence in Walker's shadow.

There was plenty of room there. Bright objects cast long, dark shadows, and Walker's light blazed. Alva's youngest son was a mystery to her. Somehow, some way, he'd managed to grow into an outgoing and exuberant boy, outside of his father's presence. Maybe it was his nature. Maybe it was a side effect of being last on the list of Silas's targets, behind his mother and older brother. Regardless of the reason, Alva prayed that Walker might have a future after this place let him go.

Eli, though. She mourned for the future Eli had sacrificed to her husband's madness. Of the two boys, Eli's meek, cowed manner should have let him fade into the background, at least sometimes. But Silas despised his eldest child, and his eyes sought Eli out, drunk or sober, watching for the least excuse to unleash a torrent of abuse. It could be anything, or nothing at all. Weakness, cowardice, stupidity . . . simply breathing the air.

Alva caught a glimpse of herself in the mirror and did a double take. Thirty-six? The woman looking back at her might have been a hundred years old. There was no resemblance to the woman she'd been raised to be.

She'd lived an entire life lessened, whittled down to tendons and regret.

Alva might have been able to find pity for the remnant of a woman in the glass. She had in the past. But today, for the first time in more years than she could remember, a spark of anger ignited, directed at the weak, impotent excuse for a human being that stared back at her. Because she'd allowed the lives of her children to be lessened too. The anger smoldered, obscuring her sight as she threw herself into the habits that made up her life. Cabinet doors slammed, cracking the silence of the house. For years, Alva had held a tight rein on her emotions. She owed the boys a gentle, steady counterpoint to Silas's moods. She'd swallowed sadness before it became tears and choked on anger until she nearly suffocated.

But today she couldn't dredge up the strength to tamp it back down one more time. It burned out of control. Today, she realized, someone would die.

Her hands came to a stop. With that thought, the fire dissipated into the bright October day. In its place, she felt frost begin to form in her arms and legs. It moved to her center, where it hardened into a solid block of ice.

If it was her, then so be it, she thought. At some unmarked point in the last year, her role as protector of her children had flipped on her. She couldn't tell you the day or the hour it had happened, but she knew with certainty their roles had reversed. Her boys stayed here and endured this existence for one reason. To protect her.

The knowledge weighed on her. How many days had her boys been at risk and how many beatings had they suffered, for her sake? Without Alva, nothing would be left to tie them here. Hope blossomed and grew, and the ice began to melt. Her boys were one precious thread away from freedom. A thread she had complete control over and the means to sever at any time.

Her own wasted life be damned. Today she'd raise a glass and toast her sons' futures—may they be as bright and free as their pasts were buried in darkness. Today would be a good day.

Walker and Eli stood in the doorway to the kitchen. Alva was smiling. Her good mood was floating around her like fairy dust.

"Mama?" Walker said.

"Walker," Alva said. "We're celebrating."

Alva loaded the kitchen table down with her day's labors. Fried chicken, creamy mashed potatoes, fresh vegetables sautéed in butter. In the middle of the table, she placed a chocolate cake, fragrant and sweet. Alva wiped her hands on her apron and surveyed the feast. She noticed the boys' hesitation and glanced up at them. Neither had moved.

"Well, don't stand there all day like a pair of old scarecrows. Sit. Eat!"

So they did, and the fear that was their constant companion slid away. Silas would be back. They all knew it. It didn't need to be said. But before he returned, they'd steal the chance to be the family they could have been.

The hours had a finality to them, though only Alva felt it. Her sons were too overcome by the sudden celebration to wonder about her motives. "Walker, honey, do you ever think about the future? What you want to do with your life, after . . ." Alva trailed off.

Alva didn't know it, but fourteen-year-old Walker dreamed about his future often. It felt so distant and unattainable, hanging like a golden carrot just out of his reach, that he'd never spoken of it.

"I want to do something that means something, Mama. Not a farmer. Something bigger." Alva took no offense. Farming was hard, full of work and worry that never seemed to fade. Often thankless, it could grind a person down. "When you figure out what that is, I want you to promise me you won't let anything stand in your way."

Alva reached across the table and grasped the hand of her young, bright boy. "Not anything or anyone. Will you promise me?"

"Sure, Mama," Walker answered, looking uneasy at his mother's tone.

"And Eli. What kind of world would you make for yourself if you could?"

Eli looked up from his plate, which he was carefully cleaning with the last of a biscuit. He looked off toward the window, his eyes glazed. Most people saw nothing there—just a boy with a mind ill equipped for the demands of existing.

She knew different. She waited, giving him the time and space he needed to put into words the pictures in his head. She studied him while he stared into the distance. His features were handsome, in spite of the slackness in his face. In the last year his voice had deepened. It still took her by surprise when she heard it. He so rarely spoke. "The woods," he said. "Quiet lives in the woods and the river. I'd live in the quiet if I could. My head doesn't hurt there. No one comes. Just quiet."

Eli focused again on his supper without a second glance. Alva blinked away tears and shook off the sadness. Regrets were useless things that had taken enough from her already.

"Can we have cake now?" Walker asked.

Alva smiled and rose to dig up some candles from the junk drawer. She found two red ones and a blue one that was bent a little, the pieces held together by the wick. Their tips were blackened and the wax on top was slightly melted. They were left over from some long-ago day, like this one, made special by its stolen moments.

She pushed the candles into the cake and lit them with the kitchen matches. The acrid smell of the match mingled with the sweetness of the chocolate and the sound of her boys singing "Happy Birthday."

Alva collected the sights, sounds, and smells of the evening, plucking each one from the air and holding it to her. The boys cleared the table and began to clean the kitchen. Alva watched them work in concert for a moment, comfortable and safe in one another's presence. Then she told them to leave it.

They glanced back at her.

"Well," she asked, "who's the mother here? I said leave it. Don't bother with that mess now. Walker, why don't you grab the radio from the cupboard and we'll put it up in the front window so we can hear it on the porch."

"But, Mama, what if . . ." Walker trailed off. They were living on borrowed time, and she knew the boys felt the pressure of the minutes passing. No one knew better how quickly this wide, beautiful day could crash around their feet.

Alva tried to settle Walker's mind. Cupping his cheek in her hand, she smiled. "Everything is gonna be fine." Something in Alva's tone must have convinced Walker the words were true.

"John Barker asked if I could sleep over tonight, Mama. Is that okay with you?"

"Well, let's talk about that. How do you feel about going on a camp-out with your brother, instead?"

And so Alva and her boys sat on the front porch, while Patsy Cline crooned about broken hearts and moonlight, and Alva said good-bye without saying good-bye.

Then she sent the boys on their way, loaded with packs of camping equipment she'd stowed for each of them earlier in the day and directions to take the truck out to the public campgrounds on the other side of town.

Alva was tempted to insist they not come back to the house for several days, no matter what, but she fought down the urge. It would make them suspicious, and she couldn't afford to have them hanging around. Not tonight.

There were no secret letters buried in the bottom of their packs, telling them of her love and explaining the reasons for her choices. Only basic supplies and the leftover cake, packaged in a tin she'd added at the last minute. Her actions would have to communicate the things she'd have liked to say.

Alva watched the taillights of the old truck wink out as the boys rumbled away, turning toward Whitewood, and she let out a pent-up breath. They had each other. They'd be fine. She had to believe that.

Later that night, Alva had done all she could think to do. Preparing for Silas to come home hadn't taken much time. Loading a gun is short work.

Her hands turned to household tasks out of a lifetime of habit, leaving her mind free to wander. With a certainty borne of nearly two decades of experience, Alva expected Silas back that night. When he stumbled home, hungover and stinking of bourbon, smoke, and rage, it would be time to settle their accounts.

Alva doubted she'd survive. Not so much had changed in the span of a day that she suddenly found herself physically stronger or more vicious than her husband. She knew her chances were slim to nonexistent. The difference was, she'd weighed her life against her children's freedom and found it laughably light, carved as hollow and empty as a jack-o'-lantern on Halloween.

But with the day gone and the silence of the night settling around her shoulders, Alva couldn't stop the nervousness from creeping in. She was willing to die so that Walker and Eli could have a future. But it wasn't her first choice. She was desperate and sadly lacking in options, but she wasn't crazy. As long as the boys were set free, a ragged life was better than none at all.

A host of potential outcomes ran through her mind. Few of them included her witnessing another sunrise, but she was bound to try. Today she'd found the woman she used to be, the woman she'd been raised to be. It wasn't in that woman's nature to do less.

Hours passed with no sign of Silas. As she sat on the porch swing, the house sparkled behind her, and the scent of lemons drifted from the open windows. The loaded rifle lay across her knees, harsh and heavy over her faded apron, but the night remained stubbornly silent.

Drifting off wasn't part of the plan. But once her body was forced into stillness, her mind couldn't help but follow. It was inevitable. Every one of Alva's senses had been wide open and thrumming throughout the day and half the night. That level of intensity is impossible to keep up forever, and as it unwound, exhaustion filled the space left behind.

Her dreams were unsettled.

When the pain came, it was sharp and blinding, cutting her ties to sleep and dropping Alva back at Silas's feet. The rifle fell to the porch with her, but it slid too far away to be anything more than a mockery. It lay forgotten on the porch, as useless as an unkept promise.

26

It was before daybreak when Eli shook Walker awake inside the tent.

"Wha . . . Eli? What's the matter?" Walker rubbed sleep from his eyes and squinted at the shape of his brother looming over him in the darkness.

"Mama's alone," Eli said. "Too happy, Walker. She was too happy to be alone with him."

It took Walker a moment to grasp Eli's meaning. They'd both been uneasy when they'd left home earlier that night, and Eli had hit on why. It wasn't unusual for Alva to send them off, but she'd never seemed pleased about the necessity of doing it.

Eli watched the understanding and the fear come alive in Walker's eyes.

"We have to go back," Walker said.

"Yes," Eli replied. "Now."

The brothers left their campsite still set up, the tent flap snapping in the wind, the remains of their campfire a dead pile of gray ash.

They left the old rusted farm truck at the turnoff onto the dirt drive that led to the only home they'd ever known.

Then they ran.

The boys were still yards from the house when the scream ripped through them as it headed in the opposite direction, barely recognizable as human. It cut Walker down midstride. He stumbled to his knees in the damp grass of the front yard. Eli stalled as well, filled with terror at the sound.

He knelt in front of Walker.

"Go back," he said, holding his brother by the forearms. Walker didn't seem to register the words, and Eli shook him, hard, leaving bruises where his fingers dug into flesh. Bruises that no one would be in any shape to notice in the coming days. They would darken, then slowly fade, unremarkable in the scheme of things.

"Walker, go back to the truck. Drive away, to any place not here," Eli said. He stood, dragging Walker up with him. He physically turned his brother around and pushed him back toward the dirt drive.

"Go, Walker," Eli hissed. Eli stood with his back to the house until he saw Walker begin to move away under his own steam, slowly at first, then running.

Then, and only then, did Eli turn and face his fate head-on. His whole life had come down to this brief and painfully sharp moment.

Eli knew the only advantage he might have was surprise. He also knew he'd long ago been beaten into a state of near-permanent submission by the man he was about to face. Submitting to Silas meant survival, by the only means available. That was a lesson he'd learned earlier than any child should, and that lesson was buried deep and true, right into the center of him. It was a barbed, rusty thing. Any attempt to pull free of it caused it to burrow deeper.

Eli also knew this fear was his greatest enemy. Not Silas himself. With sudden clarity, he realized that his father had aged. He was still strong, still dangerous. But giving yourself to drink costs more than the price of the bottle. It demands its own form of payment. Liquor had turned Silas pallid and softer than he'd ever been.

Eli knew this, just as he knew he'd grown taller, stronger, and straighter than his father. But to the trembling little boy inside him, that didn't matter. It was that little boy who was his enemy now. The boy who had long ago been conditioned to bow down, like a circus elephant that has no will to resist its keepers.

Eli forced his feet forward, one at a time. He could feel the weight of that clinging boy, whimpering in panic. He moved across the yard, then over the boards of the porch, quietly and deliberately. He pushed open the front door that was hanging ajar, and he left that boy behind, abandoned and crying silent tears, alone in the dark.

It was the cruelest, most difficult thing he'd ever done.

Things might have ended differently if Eli's timing had been better. Or maybe not. Luck had always been a stranger to Eli, so it should have come as no surprise that Silas moved to the front window at just the right moment, giving him a split-second warning that he and his unconscious wife were no longer alone.

When Eli came through the front door, his eyes locked on the body of his mother. She was lying on her side in the middle of the living room floor, naked and curled in upon herself like a child.

She was bloody, bruised, cut, and beaten. Her long dishwater hair, streaked with gray for so many years, had been hacked off around her scalp, with her skin still attached in some places, leaving raw and bloody patches.

Alva's entire body had been brutalized. Eli shouldn't have been shocked by Silas's depravity, but this broken woman lying in front of him took his breath away. Eli's nostrils flared as the stink in the room hit him. Feces. Human waste. Alva had defecated on herself. It had happened when Silas took a pine log from the wood-burning fireplace and held the glowing, crackling piece of wood to Alva's stomach. When Silas pressed the burning log into her midriff, holding it by the end the fire hadn't claimed, Alva screamed. The scream had been instinctive, involuntary, and it carried along with it any will to live she had left, leaving behind an emptied vessel.

This was the scream that had flown by her sons as they had run toward her. It faded only when their mother's mind and body shut themselves down, using the only defense left to her.

The smell that hit Eli was the same one that had sent Silas to the window. His father had planned to let some fresh air into the room, after his wife had soiled herself. Eli's stomach turned over. The smell of feces mingled with the stench of his mother's cooked flesh.

This all ran through Eli's mind in a split second, just long enough to be branded on his memory, before Silas struck from behind and blackness overtook him.

Eli floated in a nightmare world of leathery wings and poisoned talons and beaks. He regained consciousness once, when his father turned the same burning log he'd used on his mother on to him.

But before he did, Silas carefully placed the log back into the fire, letting it char and spit as the heat settled into its core. He stamped out a few stray embers that escaped onto the wooden floor, careful not to burn the place down. He laughed as he did it.

That laugh wound its way into Eli's dreams, and it was still echoing as Silas used the log to melt away half of Eli's face. Eli let out a scream of his own before falling too deeply into the dark for either laughter or nightmares to reach him.

There was no knowing how much time had passed before his mother's voice broke through. She was weeping and shaking him. Her tears were falling on his ruined face. Her voice was hoarse and slurred. Desperate.

"Eli, oh God, you can't be here. Why are you here? Eli, you have to wake up, you have to get out!"

"Mama," Eli said. He tried to close his eyes, longing to drift back into the black, but she wouldn't let him.

"Get up, Eli. You have to get out. Go, get away from him. He'll be back. He always comes back. You have to go, you have to go."

For no other reason than because his mother asked it of him, he started to rise. First, to his hands and knees, then slowly to his feet. He swayed, but stayed upright. He heard his mother say, "Go, Eli. You aren't supposed to be here."

He knew then that she had sought out a confrontation with Silas. Did she mean to die?

Eli had no words, and his mother's eyes had closed again anyway. He could only hope she was someplace where she felt nothing.

Eli fought to push past the searing wall of pain that was his face. But it was a dragon that clung to him. It had a heartbeat, and it breathed fire.

On unsteady legs, his feet moved forward. All he could do was follow along as they took him away from his mother and into the still, dark night. On the porch, Eli stooped to pick up the forgotten rifle. He nearly lost his balance then. But he knew if he did, he'd never find the strength to rise before Silas came back to kill them both. Slowly, he shuffled toward the lights and shadows thrown by another, more deadly dragon.

He stood for a single moment in the doorway of the barn. He was still swaying on his feet as Silas hummed a tune to himself while he rummaged around, then pulled out the can of diesel fuel he'd been searching for.

Eli saw him smile, and he knew Silas had plans for that fuel. If Eli couldn't stop him, then he, his mother, and the house that had never belonged to Silas would all burn bright before the night was through. Silas turned. The smile was still on his face when he looked into the eyes of a stranger, a man he'd never seen before. The rifle put an end to their nightmare with a single blast and Silas fell.

Eli barely registered the red stain blooming across his father's shirt before the black reclaimed him.

27

Walker was the one who cleaned up the mess. He'd made it as far as the truck when Eli sent him away, but he couldn't bring himself to go any farther. For hours, he waited, unsure and not knowing the right thing to do. He started back toward the house a half dozen times during the night, each time losing his nerve.

But then he heard the gunshot, and what he might be walking into or Eli's insistence he stay away didn't matter anymore. Instead, he ran, letting his feet take him home. The scene Walker entered was straight out of a nightmare. But he did what he had to do, the only thing he could have done. He took care of Eli and his mother. He bandaged their wounds, tried to set things to rights, and prayed. Eli recovered enough within a few days to regain his feet, though his face stayed under bandages for many weeks after that.

Eli should have had medical care, but secrecy was ingrained in the boys, and they were more concerned about their mother. She didn't wake up for days. When she finally did, they tried to convince her to go to the hospital, but like Eli, she refused. They didn't push her. She was their mother. They all knew that until something was done about Silas, help from anyone was out of the question. Not with Silas lying dead in the barn, wrapped in an old horse blanket soaked through with blood and pushed behind a few bales of hay.

Four days after Alva's thirty-sixth birthday, and with her blessing, her sons dug a grave for her husband and their father. Alva threw the first shovel of dirt onto the bastard herself.

The next few months were hard on what was left of the Dixon family. They knew it wasn't over yet. So they kept themselves to themselves and tried their best to heal. Alva took to wearing a hat until her hair could grow back. Eli never returned to the Whitewood public school system.

Eventually came the knock on the door they'd all been dreading.

"Mrs. Dixon?" The deputy removed his hat when Alva opened the door. He looked young.

"Yes," she said.

"I'm Deputy Willis, ma'am. From the Caddo County Sheriff's Department. Is your husband home?"

Alva had been waiting for this. She should have been nervous. She was nervous. But more than that, she was relieved the wait was over.

"No, Deputy, he's not. I'm not entirely sure where my husband is, to be honest."

The deputy glanced down at his boots, embarrassed for her. Clearly, he knew Silas's reputation. She wasn't surprised. In fact, she was counting on it.

"Well, ma'am, it's just that we've been contacted by the Cordelia police—"

"If Silas is in jail, Deputy, I've got to tell you, as far as I'm concerned, he can stay there."

"No, ma'am, that's not—"

"And you can tell that worthless excuse of a man that if he hadn't run off with the grocery money I might, just might, mind you, consider bailing him out. But as it is, I'm not feeling too generous."

Alva crossed her arms. It helped hide the trembling in her hands. She glared at the deputy, who'd backed up a step.

"No, ma'am, Mr. Dixon's not in jail," he said. "I'm just here about his car."

"His car?" she asked. "What about his car?"

"Well, ma'am, the Cordelia police reached out to us after they were contacted by a man there who owns a . . . place of business. He says that Mr. Dixon was a patron of his a few months back, and Mr. Dixon's car wouldn't start. Said it's been sitting in his lot ever since."

Alva hadn't had any idea where Silas's car was. Only that he'd shown up on the front porch as silent as a ghost. He must have hitched his way back home, then walked up the drive.

"Mr. Bowman, the proprietor, said he's going to have it towed off and sold for scrap soon, but he's had . . . dealings, we'll say, with Mr. Dixon in the past, and he's not looking for any trouble."

Alva was quiet for a moment.

"Can I ask, Deputy, just what is the nature of Mr. Bowman's place of business?"

The young man started to stammer.

"I assume, since my husband is a drunk, it's a place that sells liquor."

"Yes, ma'am," Deputy Willis said quickly, hoping that would be the end of it.

"And does it also provide, shall we say, entertainment of the female sort, for a price?"

A flush crept up the deputy's neck, and he wouldn't meet her eyes.

"I see," Alva said, holding up a hand to save him from having to answer.

"Deputy Willis, I'm not sure how to say this without sounding unchristian, but marrying Silas Dixon was the stupidest thing I've ever done. Getting drunk and getting gone are about the only two things he's good at. He's been gone long enough this time that I'm just starting to let myself hope it's gonna stick.

"So please forgive me when I say, I don't really give a damn what that man does with Silas's car. He can roll it off into the Neches for all I care. And good riddance to the car and Silas both."

She shut the door in Deputy Willis's face. Alva closed her eyes and leaned back against the door, but her legs couldn't hold her up, and she slid to the ground.

That was the last and only time the Caddo County Sheriff's Department asked about Silas Dixon.

28

The freedom, after all those years, was indescribable. In many ways, it was like someone had taken the gray out of the world. But that terrible night, and all the years before it, had taken a toll on them all. Most obviously on Eli.

Those weeks afterward, Walker cared for Eli while Alva couldn't, then Eli took over when he was able. He insisted. Alva didn't see the full extent of what Silas had done to him until the bandages came off for good.

When she did, the sight of the scarred ruin of Eli's face caused a visceral reaction. She broke out in a sweat, then started to tremble. She tried to hold it back, knowing Eli could see on her face everything she was feeling, but the harder she tried, the worse it got. Holding back sobs, Alva ran for the bathroom, barely making it in time to turn out the contents of her stomach.

It wasn't disgust or aversion. It was the opposite. All Alva wanted was to fix it for him, to make it undone. It was the one thing she could never do, and it tore her up inside.

Alva tried to hide her feelings, to not let them show. It was one more burden to place on Eli, but she couldn't hold the emotions back, no matter how hard she tried. Not for years.

Eli would catch her staring at him, transfixed by his scars. Then a sheen of sweat would break out across her face and her hands would start to shake. Before long she'd be physically sick. It hurt him. Alva knew it did. She watched him take it in with a growing sadness.

Seeing Eli accept it as his due, as no more than he should expect, intensified Alva's reaction. When she looked on the destruction of her son's face—recognizing the innocent child she'd brought into a world of pain and abuse that he'd never asked for, that no child deserves—she saw her own failure. A failure so complete it brought her to her knees. It left her debilitated in a much deeper place than Silas had ever managed to touch. And instead of pulling herself together to be the mother her son needed her to be, she let it break her. She failed him again.

Eli and Walker built the camp house on the riverbank together. They said it was a place for Eli to be alone in the quiet, away from the memories the house held. They said it was temporary, a place to use when Eli needed space.

But Alva knew Eli was giving her the one thing he had in his power to give. He was giving her the gift of his absence. The first night he spent alone down by the river, she knew he'd never return to live in their house, knew they'd never all live there as a whole family again.

She knew, and she still let him go. She never forgave herself for that.

The years passed and Alva told herself he'd found peace there, in a place where pain couldn't find him. That he'd become part of the woods he'd immersed himself in. Sometimes she even let herself believe it. But mostly she knew that on the night they buried Silas, they'd built a cage for all of them. One they could never break free of.

Alva's boys, and Eli in particular, took up their posts standing guard over Silas's grave. They did it for her. They knew they'd never leave this place, not for long. Walker left for a time, then returned with Winnie, who was her own kind of broken.

In her attempt to give her sons their freedom, Alva had tied them tighter than ever to this place.

2012

Alva's eyes were haunted and her hands trembled when she turned and met her granddaughter's gaze across the kitchen table. "I'm telling you this because I need you to know that I understand the need to protect your child. And I know, from a deep and true place, that Eli has no malice in him. He simply isn't capable of harming another living thing.

"I would never ask you to place Kate in harm's way. Not for my sake and not for the sake of my son. I would rather die. You've kept your child safe in a way I wasn't capable of. It's the greatest thing a mother can achieve. And you've done it. I would never ask you to compromise that.

"All I'm asking, Hadley, is that you give Eli a chance to explain. Please, I'm begging you, from one mother to another. Can you, *will* you do that for me?"

29

Hadley considered her grandmother. She could see the tenuous balancing act Gran was performing. The son she couldn't heal. The granddaughter she couldn't reassure. The great-granddaughter she couldn't protect. And the past that had poisoned them all.

"I can, Gran. I will. I'll give him a chance to explain. And I hope you're right. But if you're wrong . . ."

Eli was no longer a boy protecting his mother. He was a damaged, reclusive man who'd grown in tainted soil. It was no indication of innocence.

"There's more to this than either of you know. I think it's time to go talk to Eli," Jude said, looking grim and pale but determined to see this through.

The three women walked together down the wooded path toward Eli's place. Hadley felt almost like she was walking into a fairy-tale land. The day began to lose its sense of place and time. Sounds of the world fell away, muffled by woods and water and magic. The sun tried to push its way through the tall trees, but it was a tough job. By the time the light ended its journey to the earth, it was strewn upon the path like broken glass.

When Jude spoke, her words circled around them in their wooded cocoon, and Hadley tried to shake off the sensation that the living things around them were all pieces of a whole. That the woods were listening, judging their worthiness to continue on this path.

"Eli and I . . . we've become friends . . . of a sort. I visit him here sometimes. And he leaves gifts for me, at my home. A morning glory vine, twisted around a tree branch. Fish from the river, swimming in an old cooler with no lid. Once, a long time ago, he brought me a basket of pecans . . ." Jude's voice drifted off.

Hadley had questions, so many questions, clamoring for answers. She forced them to line up and wait their turn. She knew this wasn't the time or place to push. Not when explanations waited ahead, luring them farther and deeper in.

Gran was quiet too. Hadley could see she was thrown off balance by Jude's words. Surprised, maybe, that she and Walker weren't his only links to the outside. Hadley wondered what other secrets he might have kept from his mother. Eli hadn't been a boy for a very long time, if he'd ever been one. How well can a mother know the man her son grows up to be?

When the women arrived at Eli's home, each was lost in her own anxiety about what was coming. As they approached the weathered shack by the river, Hadley spotted a mockingbird sitting in the branches of a scrub oak. It was silent and watchful. She knew from her own child-hood in these woods that mockingbirds were territorial. They could be aggressive if you wandered too near their nest. She wondered if this one was measuring their steps, watching to see if they would cross an invisible line and become a threat to her young.

Rest easy, little one, she thought. *We're not here to hurt your babies.*

Eli's home would look tumbledown to most. It was small, unadorned, and unassuming. The boards were a raw pine turned gray with age, and there were patched places along the exterior walls. The materials used for repairs hadn't been chosen for looks, surely scavenged lumber from whatever might be at hand.

There was no paint, and there were no flower boxes or sparkly clean windows. Hadley saw a place near the east corner that had been mended with what could only be duct tape, judging from the dull gray sheen and the withered white edges that rolled back in places.

But in spite of all that, or because of it, there was beauty here. A magnificence of the kind found in the creased, leathery faces of old men full of tall tales and tobacco-stained teeth.

This shack, this home, could have grown here. It could have sprouted out of the east Texas riverbank soil, fertilized by pine needles and motor oil, raised with loving, calloused hands by trailer park mothers who smelled like cinnamon and menthol cigarettes. It was a part of this place, indigenous in a way that pretty, air-conditioned new construction could never be.

Hadley now knew why Eli had chosen this, this life removed. Alva and her boys had buried their husband and father here. Their dirty little secret. That was what chained Eli to this place.

He was standing guard, making sure that both Silas's body and Silas's ghost remained exactly where they'd put him.

Hadley was shaken from her reverie when Jude knocked on Eli's door, breaking the stillness that had settled around them. But the haunting, fairy-tale feel of the day remained when the door creaked open.

"Eli," Jude said in a gentle voice. "Eli, it's time. Your mother and Hadley are here with me, and you need to tell them what you told me. You need to tell them about Cooper."

Hadley was holding her breath. For a moment, no one spoke. She thought Eli might slam the door in Jude's face. Some part of her hoped he would.

But then Eli let the door swing open and he stepped out. It had been many years since Hadley had seen Eli up close. She remembered being repelled by him as a child. He'd been the embodiment of her nightmares, with his scars and his aloof ways. Every scary story told with flashlights under the covers or by the light of a campfire had taken on Eli's form. He'd been the hook man, the werewolf, and the headless horseman, blended into one. As he stepped into the soft light of the day, Hadley recognized how that fear had taken root. Eli's scars were hideous, even to an adult's eyes. They left his skin discolored and rearranged, ridged and puckered where it should have been smooth and smooth where it shouldn't be. His ruined face had healed in a way that pulled his left eye into a permanent droop, like it too was about to melt and slide down his cheek.

And yet, even as Hadley saw that her child's view hadn't been exaggerated, she couldn't help but recognize more on his face than she'd expected.

She saw fear.

Eli's eyes flitted back and forth between Jude and his mother like a wild, wounded creature who'd been caught in a trap.

Hadley felt an overwhelming sense of shame as it occurred to her that she'd never, not once in her life, taken the time to recognize that this man was a person. She tried to tell herself it didn't matter, that this confrontation, or whatever it was, wasn't about Eli, or about her. It was about Kate. She held that thought to her like a talisman, but her shame didn't fade.

Hadley could see Jude struggle to find the right words to put Eli at ease. She took both of the big man's rough hands into her own.

"Eli, Hadley is worried for Kate. She thinks you're a danger to her daughter."

Eli glanced Hadley's way, but he couldn't hold her gaze. Instead he bowed his head, his hands still in Jude's. The silent moment dragged on as they watched Eli struggle with himself.

After what felt like centuries, he looked up into Jude's face. Hadley was shocked to see tears on his cheeks.

"You'll stay?" he asked Jude.

"Of course I'll stay," she said, her voice breaking as she blinked away tears of her own. "I'm not going anywhere."

Eli's home was too small to hold all of them or the tale he had to tell, so they sat on the grass by the bank of the river and Eli told them the truth about Cooper Abbott's last day. Eli's words were halting at first. Hadley could see why people believed he was slow. He spoke in the same way he saw the world, raw and blunt.

But eventually, her ears adjusted to the choppy cadence of his speech, and his rusty baritone flowed over her with an almost natural rhythm. A song in half time, full of minor chords.

"Boy was fishing. Right down there. A fool thing. Fish are lazy. Look for coves and food slower than them. Ain't no fish fighting the current. They're sleeping. Boy should have been sleeping too."

Eli's eyebrows drew together, and he shook his head.

"But the sun rose and found the boy first thing, hair shining like a new copper penny. Looked like a angel. But he weren't no angel. Just a boy. A angel'd know that's no place to find fish."

Hadley thought of Cooper, really thought, for the first time in many years. She remembered his fearlessness, his fascination with a golden fish that could grant wishes.

"Watched the boy. Told the sheriff I never seen him that day, but I lied. Thought of the day before. Didn't see nobody that day, so a lie felt like a truth. But it weren't true. Was a lie. I watched the copper-headed boy. Saw him trying to catch fish where there weren't none. That boy was the only thing got caught on the river that morning. The angel boy with the copper hair."

Hadley shivered in spite of the bright sun. She looked away from Eli then and watched the ripples on the river flash in the sun. It made her think of cameras flashing, collecting images and emotions from her face that she didn't care to show the world. She closed her eyes and laid her forehead on her knees, keeping her thoughts hidden from the prying eyes of the river as Eli continued.

"I mostly stand well back from folks 'less I got something to say. They scared of me. It's okay, most times. Don't care much for folks anyway. And sometimes folks need to be scared. Like that boy. I'd done tried scaring him away before. Him and you girls." Eli shook his head again.

"Didn't listen. Was a mistake. I thought maybe I ought to scare him again, but I didn't want to ruin the fool boy's morning. Was a bigger mistake. Biggest one of all."

Eli trailed off, staring at the place downriver where the water disappeared around a bend. "Thought the boy was safe. Moved upriver, back up into the trees. Had some things needed tending."

Hadley wondered what things Eli tended but kept her thoughts to herself. Eli's willingness to speak was shaky, and she could sense that interruptions would upset his balance. Besides, what did it matter?

"When I stepped back out of the woods, the boy was gone. Thought he gave up, went home. I wasn't in no hurry. Wouldn't have mattered if I was. Too late by then. I headed back here, making my way slow-like. Pretty morning, I recall. Quiet. Wasn't till I got closer that I heard the crying. Coming from up there."

Eli pointed northward up the river to a place Hadley remembered. It was the clearing where she'd sketched, so long ago, while her friends had lazed by the water, telling tales. It was Dixon land, but everyone knew Alva didn't begrudge anyone access to the river, as long as they carted out everything they brought in with them. Some of the locals would use it from time to time, but it was near enough to Eli's shack and the woods he inhabited that most people avoided it altogether. The Neches was a long river, and there were plenty of places to fish that weren't haunted by the bogeyman.

"Had a bad feeling," Eli continued. "Couldn't see the boy. Hoped real hard he'd gone on home, but I knew he didn't. Came on the spot, real quiet-like, hoping for . . . Don't know what for. No bad things. But that crying, it chilled my bones. I come 'round the corner, slow. And he's there."

Hadley didn't want to hear this. Only the thought of Kate kept her from running home and never looking back.

"He hurt that boy. Hurt him real bad. Said he didn't mean to kill him. Didn't mean for it to happen. He was scared. Scared and sorry. But sorry don't mean nothing to a dead boy. Sorry's just a word. Was too late to fix it. So I gathered that copper-headed boy up, while he sat there crying tears into the dirt. The day wasn't so pretty no more. Storm clouds gathering."

Eli stopped and looked at his mama, who was silent and pale.

"I tried to do right by him, Mama. Best I could. Gathered up that boy. Put his clothes to rights, and I carried him till I found a quiet place. A pretty place.

"Saw Winnie along the way. Thought she might scream, me with a dead boy and all. But she smiled. She smiled and kissed his cheek. Called him Johnny, and walked back the way she'd come."

Eli shook his head.

"Your mama, child . . . But that ain't here nor there."

Alva was crying silent tears. "I dug his grave real deep, hoping he'd rest easy away from the badness and hurt in the world. I buried him with his fishing pole. Figured where he'd gone, maybe the fish always bite."

Eli gestured to a shady place in the trees. "He's buried right over there, that copper-haired boy. Right by the cove, I put him. That's where the fish stay. Deep in the weeds, sleeping."

Eli fell silent. No one spoke. No one wanted to be the first to break the spell his words had spun, and the moment stretched. But the question had to be asked. It was floating around them like a foul smell that they were all too scared to name. "Why, Eli?" Hadley forced the words past her lips. It was the first time she'd spoken since they'd left the kitchen at the farmhouse. Her voice was quiet, but she had to know.

"Why didn't you tell anyone? Why keep it a secret all this time?" she asked.

Eli didn't meet her eyes.

"I let that boy down, and one day I gotta answer for that. Should have gone back and killed him. Choked the life out of him until he was dead and put his bones in the ground next to Silas. But I couldn't do it. I was too late to help that boy, but I didn't want to see nobody else hurt."

Hadley could see the tension around Eli's neck and shoulders, the way he wouldn't meet anyone's eyes.

But she'd stepped too far onto this ledge. There was no way back, and only one way forward. "Who, Eli? Who were you protecting? Who was the man?"

Eli's eyes were full of sorrow when they met Hadley's. But sorry would never be enough. *Sorry's* nothing but a word.

"You. I was protecting you, girl. Mama too, but you most of all. 'Cause nothing hurts so bad as that first notion that the world ain't hardly ever the way it ought to be."

Hadley could feel her world come untethered.

"But why? Why me?" she whispered.

"I knew it weren't going to stop. Should have killed him. But I couldn't do it. He's my brother. My brother and your daddy."

There was a hissing in Hadley's head as a lit match was dropped on the trail of gasoline Eli's words had left there. She saw the fire catch and race away, out of her control. She watched, helpless, as it formed the shape of her father, burning in effigy. Hadley barely heard Eli when he continued. He was looking back at the river.

"It was the anniversary, see. That's a real pretty word, *anniversary*, to mark such a day. Four days after Mama's birthday. The day we put Daddy in the ground. Walker, he stank of liquor. Took me aback. Walker don't drink, so far as I knew. But it was a liquor stink all the same. Maybe he was toasting our daddy in hell."

Hadley felt numb, detached from the world. But reality crashed in at the sound of her grandmother's voice.

"Nooo," Alva cried. "Eli, that's not true. You tell me that's not true! Eli?"

In spite of Alva's denial, her words didn't have the sharpness of a true disbeliever. Eli said nothing more, only held his mother when she crumpled in on herself. But Alva wasn't defending Walker's innocence. She was keening in the mournful way of a mother standing over the broken body of a lost child.

Hadley couldn't look away. It was like watching a mended vase that had been painstakingly put back together shatter all over again because the first piece had been set poorly.

That's when it happened.

Alva tensed, her cries suddenly cut short.

If the muscles of her face were held up by strings, someone had come along and clipped half of them in one go. "Mama?" Eli asked. They all realized at the same time that something was very, very wrong.

Eli picked up his mother and cradled her in his arms.

"Can you carry her to the house?" Hadley asked, near panic. He didn't reply, just took off at a run with fear in his eyes. Hadley and Jude were right behind him.

The time they spent waiting for the ambulance to arrive was torture. Eli held his mother, refusing to put her down, rocking her like a child. Kate was back at the house, and Hadley hated the fear she saw in her child's eyes.

"I'll take her over to my mom," Jude said. Vivienne Monroe still lived across the road, next door to Charlotte Abbott, and Hadley knew she'd take care of Kate like one of her own. Hadley nodded. "Thank you," she said, then watched them go: her oldest friend, her daughter, and her daughter's dog trailing at their feet. Her world.

Hadley felt each second ticking by. She'd been to hell and back a half dozen times that day. She wondered if this last trip was going to be one-way.

Alva was scared and grief-stricken. You could see it in her eyes. But she was silent. Then she grew agitated. She reached out a hand for Hadley, who knelt next to her.

"Hadley," she said, her voice odd. Speech was difficult, but she persisted. "Did your daddy ever . . . Oh God, Hadley, did he ever hurt you?"

"No! No, Gran! Daddy never, ever hurt me!" Hadley wanted to reassure her grandmother and reassure herself. And it wasn't a lie. He'd never laid a hand on her, never looked at her with anything other than love and pride.

Alva nodded, then squeezed her eyes closed. The tears fell, traveling down the path made by the wrinkles at the corners of her eyes. Hadley had always thought of those wrinkles as smile lines, but she could see then they were vessels. Sometimes, when life let them, they held happiness. But happiness hadn't carved them there, and happiness wasn't around that day.

30

"Here," Jude said, handing Hadley a cup of coffee. It was late. Gran had been whisked away long ago, somewhere within the rabbit warren of hospital rooms and corridors behind swinging doors. There'd been a brief visit by an impossibly young doctor to explain to them that Hadley's grandmother had had a stroke. They were performing emergency surgery to attempt to repair the bleeding in her brain. There were larger, more technical terms tossed around in there, but Hadley fixated on the phrase "bleeding in the brain" and heard little after that.

That had been hours ago, and each minute since then had hobbled by on blistered, dragging feet.

Hadley took the coffee, thankful and worn thin.

"I need to call my father," Hadley said, avoiding her friend's eyes. She stared at her shoes instead. *These look like a librarian's shoes,* she thought in surprise, ugly and utilitarian. *How had this happened?* she wondered. When had she become a woman who wore practical shoes?

"I can't do it. Not yet. He needs to know, but I . . . I can't bear to hear his voice right now. I need answers. So many answers to so many questions. How did we get here, Jude?"

Jude sighed and rubbed the exhaustion from her eyes.

"Let's go find someplace a little more private, Hadley. We need to talk. We may as well do it now."

After asking an uninterested orderly where they could find a little privacy, they were directed to the hospital chapel.

The place was deserted. Hadley wasn't particularly religious. If pressed on the subject she would admit to a certain spirituality. But it was a kind that felt out of place and underdressed in a church.

Jude, though, had been raised Catholic and seemed comfortable lighting a candle and kneeling before the large figure of Christ upon the cross that dominated the front of the small chapel. Hadley followed her friend's lead, even though the gestures felt awkward.

Unbidden and unwelcome, she remembered a tasteless joke one of her husband's coworkers had drunkenly told at a party. Something about finding Jesus in the trunk of his car as he crossed the border from Mexico. The joke hadn't been funny then, though the old roughneck had laughed uproariously at his own wit. It still wasn't funny, but Hadley had to stifle a hysterical and highly inappropriate giggle. The two women took seats side by side in an oak pew.

"You never asked me how Eli and I came to be friends," Jude said. Her voice was quiet, even though they had the chapel to themselves. In spite of Hadley's mild discomfort at their surroundings, she was glad they weren't seated in the hospital cafeteria, with its brown plastic chairs, the buzzing fluorescent lights, and the aroma of institutional food floating around them.

"No," she said. "I didn't. Will you tell me?" she asked.

"I will. I'll tell you everything. But let's not start there. Let's start with Eli and Walker . . . and Silas."

"How do you . . . ?"

"From Eli. Bits and pieces, shared over many years. I don't know it all, but I can tell you what I do know."

1969

Eli and Alva had both believed that Eli was Silas's victim of choice. And it was true that every blow he landed on his eldest son must have given him twice the satisfaction, knowing it was also a blow directly to his wife's weakest spot. But what they didn't know was that Silas found a sick satisfaction in abusing his younger son, Alva's golden boy, in private.

Walker was seven years old the first time Silas crept into his room. It was five long years before anyone knew.

On the night Eli discovered the darkest secret a house filled with nightmares can hold, he was fourteen and he'd taken a beating that day. His head was pounding like a drum line, and he couldn't rest. He snuck down into the kitchen and rummaged quietly and desperately in the drawer where his mama kept the headache powders, hoping for even a moment of relief.

It was rare for Eli to be out of bed at night. He'd learned that lesson when he was three years old. Plagued by dark, scary dreams, he'd gone searching for his mother. He found Silas first, who'd taught him what happened to little boys who got out of their beds at night.

He could still remember the sounds of his mama screaming at Silas to stop, crying that he was just a boy, just a baby, while she pounded on the door Silas had locked behind them. Her terrified begging whipped Silas's fury higher. It was a lesson Eli never forgot.

On silent feet, Eli moved back to his room, avoiding the squeaky floorboard as he passed the door to the room where his father slept. He was still near the bottom of the stairs when he saw his brother's door at the top begin to open. He nearly gave himself away and whispered for Walker to "shh, stay quiet."

He managed to pull the words back just in time when he saw his father emerging from the room. Quickly, he ducked around the staircase as Silas came down. Silas never glanced Eli's way. He was busy buttoning his pants.

Once Silas had gone into his own downstairs bedroom and shut the door behind him, Eli took the stairs two at a time up to Walker's room. Eli's hand touched the cold brass of Walker's doorknob, then stalled.

He could hear muffled sobs coming from behind the door. He instinctively knew his brother wouldn't want Eli to see him like this. Instead, he slowly turned toward his own room. He lay awake for the rest of the night, staring at his ceiling, thoughts of sleep long gone.

At breakfast the next day, with Silas still sleeping, as was his habit, Eli told his mama and brother that he needed Walker to sleep in his room with him.

They both looked at him in surprise.

"Is something wrong?" Alva asked with a wary expression on her face. "Been sleepwalking," Eli told them. "Woke up in the yard last night and didn't know how I come to be there. If Walker's there he can stop me before I walk off into the river."

Walker scrutinized his brother's face, but Eli held it blank as he finished mopping up the rest of his biscuits and gravy.

That day, after Silas made his way out of the house to work his way through a bottle of bourbon, they moved Walker's mattress to Eli's floor.

Late that night, while the brothers were each pretending to be asleep, they could hear the faint sounds of Silas finding his way to Walker's door. Both boys held their breath. Moments later, they jumped, two hearts hammering in the dark, as their father softly drummed his fingers against Eli's locked door.

The lock was laughable—a bit of brass that slid into the wood of the doorjamb. It wouldn't even put up a decent fight if Silas decided he wanted past. But instead of forcing his way in, Silas chuckled, then walked down the hallway, whistling his favorite tune. Eli and Walker both let their breath out. Eli allowed himself a moment of relief that his plan had worked, at least for the night. Because he didn't think his story about sleepwalking had fooled Walker for a minute.

But he couldn't get the sound of that tune out of his head. The two didn't speak of it, and Eli was cautiously optimistic. Moving Walker into his room seemed to have worked. Walker was free of Silas's nighttime visits. He should have known better.

It was four days before Silas found an opportunity he'd been waiting for. He laughed softly as he slipped his hand across Walker's mouth and pulled him into the barn. It was broad daylight.

Eli believed Walker began to have . . . urges. Urges he couldn't control, even before Silas died. There was a boy from town, a young boy Walker took under his wing. The boy was excited to be included with Walker's older crowd of friends. He had a bad case of hero worship. Starry-eyed, almost.

At first, Eli didn't give the friendship much thought. Walker, somehow, was able to live a life separate from their father. The harder Silas tried to taint his son, the brighter Walker's light shone. Or so it seemed.

Then one day after school, Eli saw the boy coming out of the woods behind the farmhouse, alone. He was moving quickly, almost running. He saw Eli watching him and an expression full of fear and shame washed over his face. Then he did run, grabbing up his bicycle and peddling away.

Eli saw Walker slowly walk out of the woods moments later. He called his brother's name, but Walker pretended not to hear him, moving off in the opposite direction.

Walker was quiet that night, withdrawn to the degree that Alva asked him at dinner if he was coming down with something.

"Yeah, maybe," Walker said, avoiding her eyes. He asked to be excused.

Eli wondered if that boy had been lucky enough to find some comfort once he made it home, or if he'd realized already that no matter how hard he searched, the comfort he was hoping to find would slip from his fingers.

With a profound sense of loss, Eli stepped into the role of his brother's keeper. He kept watch, looking for signs Walker might be cultivating a closeness with anyone younger than himself. Others noticed Eli often trailed in his brother's wake, and people thought it was strange, but Eli didn't have the luxury of caring what the people of Whitewood whispered about him.

Long periods of time passed without incident. Sometimes Eli doubted his impression of what he'd seen that day with the boy in the woods. What if he was wrong, casting Walker in such a damning light? But deep inside his gut, where true things lived, he knew he wasn't wrong.

Walker knew his brother watched him. Eli made sure of that. Most of the time, Eli's presence seemed to help him keep his darker inclinations in check, buried under the weight of his brother's gaze. But there were a few times, over the years, that Walker slid beneath Eli's watchful vigil. Eli could count these times on one hand, but the fact that they didn't happen often didn't make them easier to bear when he was alone by the river and the ghosts came knocking on his door.

When Walker left Whitewood as a young man, intent to make something more of his life, Eli was worried. He couldn't leave this place. He had to stay, to keep the bones of his father from creeping up and out of the depths they'd sent him to. Eli believed, to the marrow of his own bones, that if given even a moment's grace, Silas would find a way to devour Alva, even from the grave.

So with an anxious heart, Eli watched his brother drive away from Whitewood, determined to make a fresh start. He hoped Walker would find a way to put his demons to rest, because Eli couldn't be there to help wrestle them down.

Underneath the worry, there was also an unbidden sense of relief.

In time, light began to flicker in Alva's eyes, and Eli tried to find peace in the world around him. When Walker came back to Whitewood with his damaged wife in tow, Alva blossomed. Her bright boy had returned. Winnie might be dragging around her own set of ghosts, but then, weren't they all?

One day Walker told his mother, "We're going to have a baby, Mama." Eli watched Alva's eyes brighten. A grandchild. She would have a grandchild. For the first time since Silas's death, Eli could see hope on her face. Whatever twisted game Silas had forced them to play, his mother seemed to believe they'd won.

But Eli said nothing when he heard the news. He was afraid if he opened his mouth, the dread that was filling him would pour out and drown them all.

31

The hospital chapel swallowed up Jude's words, leaving silence in their wake. Hadley was having a hard time absorbing the blows.

"My daddy never touched me," Hadley whispered, repeating the words she'd said to her grandmother. Jude gave her a sad smile.

"I know that, Hadley," she said and left it at that. "Why don't I go see if there's been any word on Alva's condition? Then I'll call and check on Kate, too," Jude said.

"Okay," Hadley replied, barely audible. Lost inside her own head, she hardly noticed when her friend moved away, leaving her with only her thoughts and an oversize messiah for company.

When Jude returned, she came with more coffee and good news. Alva's surgery had gone well, and she'd been moved into intensive care. The doctor couldn't say much more until she woke and he could get a better idea of how much damage the stroke had done. Until then, he suggested they go home and get some rest.

Hadley found herself short of breath, and her hands had begun to tremble.

"Jude, I . . . I don't know what to do now. I can't go home. Not yet. I'm not ready . . ."

"Of course you're not going home," Jude said. "You're coming with me. I'm going to take you to Mama's. Mateo and I have a house just up the road, but Mama Viv is going to take care of you. She insisted, so if you have a problem with that, you'll have to take it up with her."

Hadley felt tears backing up behind her eyes, but she didn't argue. The two women climbed into Jude's car and made the drive back to Whitewood. Hadley was overwhelmed. She was barely functioning, but for now all that mattered was that her grandmother was in good hands, and she was on her way to her daughter.

Vivienne welcomed Hadley warmly and without questions, and Hadley climbed into bed next to her daughter and slept.

Kate woke her the next morning. Vivienne had sent her in with fresh coffee and an offer of crepes filled with strawberries and cream. Hadley felt a sharp and unwanted pang of jealousy, wondering what it must have been like growing up with a mother like Vivienne. She pushed away the thought. It was petty.

She'd had Gran. Gran and Walker had provided all the things her mother hadn't been able to give.

The thought of her father sliced Hadley's heart open all over again.

She'd have to face him soon. She wasn't ready. She'd never be ready.

Jude and a dark, handsome man were seated at the breakfast table when Hadley joined them.

"Hadley, this is my husband, Mateo," Jude said. "He and I went by your house this morning and got some things you might need, and we brought over your car." Jude nodded toward an overnight bag on the floor. Hadley could have cried all over again at the gesture, but she refused to start so early in the day. Instead she swallowed the tears and said, "Thank you."

"No one was home," Jude said, answering the unspoken question. "But I walked down to the river and caught Eli up on his mother's condition." Hadley had forgotten about Eli. "Hey, kiddo," Mateo said to Kate, "I've got an idea. Since these ladies are going to head to the hospital later, how about you give me a hand around here today?"

Kate looked up from where she'd been sneaking a piece of bacon to the puppy under the table. "Doing what?" she asked, swallowing a mouthful of whipped cream.

"Mama Viv's been asking me if I could get around to painting her house. I figure, if you're willing to help, I could knock it out in half the time."

Kate's face lit up.

"Oh, Mom, can I please? I mean, I'll come to the hospital and see Gran with you if you want me to, though."

Kate's struggle was so clearly etched on her face that Hadley had to smile.

"Honey, Gran may not even wake up today, but if she does, I'll be sure to give her your love. If you want to stay here and do some manual labor, then by all means, feel free."

Kate beamed. "Oh, thank you! I promise I'll come with you on the next trip. I can't believe I get to help paint a whole house!" She turned to Vivienne. "What color do you want it painted, Miss Vivienne?"

Vivienne Monroe wasn't a fanciful woman. Her house had been off-white since the day it got its first coat of paint. When Joseph Monroe was alive, he'd freshened it up every two or three years. He knew she didn't like it to look dingy.

But it was five years gone now since her husband's heart attack. She still reached for him every morning in the bed during those hazy moments before the memories came back.

"Purple, I think," she said.

Every pair of eyes at the breakfast table widened and turned to her. Kate's face was filled with what could only be awe.

"Really?" Kate breathed in the way that only young girls can. *"Really?"* Jude echoed. Her tone was entirely different. "Yes, really," Vivienne said serenely, acting for all the world like those words hadn't slipped out of her mouth just to make a little girl happy.

"The question is, what shade? Kate, I'm going to need your help with that, honey. Should I go with a pale lavender, or maybe a plum? Or darker, an aubergine?"

"What's aubergine?" Kate asked, and Hadley couldn't help but smile. Kate's awe was clearly deepening at the idea that Miss Vivienne might paint her house a color she'd never even heard of. And one with such a fancy name, at that. "It's French for pain in my ass," Mateo said, earning a smack in the arm from his wife and a glare from his mother-in-law.

"Butt, I meant to say," he corrected, but Kate took no notice of him.

Kate threw her arms around her mother and said, "Give that to Gran when she wakes up, okay? And tell her I love her, and I miss her, and I want her to come home real soon. And tell her I get to help paint Miss Vivienne's house purple today, okay? Thanks, Mom!" And she was off like a shot, Buttercup giving a bark of approval and bouncing after the girl.

"Oh my God," Hadley said. "She's never been so excited in her life. Thank you, Vivienne. And thank you too, Mateo. I hope you know what you're getting yourself into."

Mateo sent her a warm smile.

"You don't need to thank me, dear," Vivienne said. "As soon as I woke up this morning I thought to myself, There is nothing I want more than a purple house." She turned to Mateo and clapped her hands. "Now get up and go help the girl, you good-for-nothing son-in-law."

"Yes, ma'am," Mateo said with a salute.

"Now," Vivienne continued, taking charge of the day like a woman who'd raised six children and buried a husband. "Hadley, you go on back and take a shower and put some color on your face. You're so pale that if you show up at the hospital like that they're gonna hunt up an extra bed and keep you."

Hadley smiled and did as she was told, although she couldn't leave the kitchen without catching Vivienne in a hug.

"Go on now," Viv said, a hitch in her voice.

"Yes, ma'am," Hadley said.

"Jude, girl, as for you, you're on kitchen cleanup duty with me."

"Yes, ma'am," came Jude's reply. You didn't argue with Vivienne Monroe. It would be as pointless as spitting in the face of a storm.

By the time Hadley emerged, she felt nearly human again. Vivienne had sent Mateo and Kate off to the hardware store to have paint mixed, and she'd installed Jude on the front porch with two glasses of iced tea and a bowl of pears that needed to be cored and peeled if she was going to make Kate the fresh pear cake she had planned. Then she'd disappeared back into the house, claiming she had things that needed doing, and giving the two women some privacy.

Hadley took a seat next to Jude on the porch swing Dr. Monroe had hung from the rafters back when he and Vivienne had been so young. Picking up the spare paring knife and a bright, ripe pear, she set to helping her friend. She could see the Abbott house in the distance.

"I called over to the hospital. Alva hasn't woken up, but they said that was to be expected and there was no cause to worry yet," Jude told her.

"Thank you," Hadley said. They worked side by side in silence for a while before Hadley spoke again.

"You never did tell me how you and Eli came to be friends."

"No, I guess I didn't," Jude said. "We'll get there soon enough."

But she said nothing more.

A long time passed, and then she began.

32

Eli was relieved when Hadley was born. A girl. For some reason he'd never considered it might be a girl. Yet there she was. Quiet and new, she lay in Walker's arms with a head full of dark hair and eyes that blinked at the world like it might be an interesting place to see.

Eli wouldn't go near her. "Walker, this ain't no place for a babe," he told his brother when Walker showed up with the little bundle. Eli backed away until he couldn't back any more, bumping into his makeshift bed.

The place had never felt small to Eli before, but suddenly, his arms and legs wouldn't fit into the space. He circled the cabin, his back to the walls, until the open door was behind him. Then he could breathe again.

To Eli, little Hadley Dixon might as well have been an alien. He had no experience with a small person whose heart and soul were still intact. It was intimidating, like being asked to handle a precious artifact from a lost civilization. If you break it, it's gone from the world forever, the last of its kind.

Walker didn't seem to be bothered by his brother's discomfort. He was too enthralled with his daughter's face. "She's perfect, Eli," he said. "She's a miracle. A little piece of me and Winnie, the best pieces. Whole pieces."

Eli was happy for his brother, but he wondered where Walker thought he'd found a whole piece of himself to pass along to this new life. From all appearances, the child had turned Walker into a new man, one who took to fatherhood like it was a role he had been born to. It was a shame motherhood didn't sit as easy on Winnie.

From the time Winnie arrived in Whitewood, she'd wandered into the trees by the river when the mood took her. Eli didn't know her story, but he quickly saw she was a person looking for . . . something. He could understand that.

But where the woods had given Eli nearly all he could need, Winnie was too lost in her own head for the trees and river to be her saving grace. She was drawn to them anyway.

"Hello," Winnie would say when she spied Eli, always sounding like he was an old friend she'd run into on the street, in spite of the fact that their encounters took place in the moonlight with Winnie's nightgown floating around her ankles and bare feet.

"Did you know I'm going to Nashville?" she'd asked him on the first night he found her wandering alone through the pines. He wanted to keep his distance but needed to make sure she was safe.

"That so?" Eli asked.

"Oh yes, I've already got my bus ticket." The moon was shining off Winnie's face as she closed her eyes and tilted her head up to drink it in like it was a spotlight on the stage of the Grand Ole Opry. Then she started to sing.

She sang "Old Rugged Cross," and her voice was sweet and clear as it floated up and away into the night, a perfect white dove released in a place it didn't belong and couldn't stay.

"I like gospel," Winnie told him. "It makes me feel like God was there for somebody. When I sing gospel I can almost believe again. But then the song ends."

Some nights Winnie would wander to the river and sing for hours, ignoring Eli completely while he watched from a distance. Winnie could sing like an angel crying when she wanted to, but when she turned to the blues, that was when she had real power. The sound resonated down into the earth around her, traveling deep and far. When Winnie sang the blues, it was mournful and moaning, and it made Eli wonder what her soul looked like under the disguise of a young, lost girl. He often found tears on his cheeks once her songs were done. Some nights she'd talk to him. Eli would come close enough to hear her words but never all the way out of the shadows. She didn't seem to care that he rarely spoke back.

She talked about blues singers, dead and gone. She told him about Blind Willie Jackson, whose stepmother had thrown lye in his face when he was seven because his daddy had beaten her for stepping out on him. Winnie said his singing had started a riot in New Orleans when he was a boy. When she sang her version of "Trouble Will Soon Be Over," he could see why.

Gospel blues was all edges, nobody bothering to smooth them over with politeness or false hope. The only hope in the blues that Winnie sang was a hope for better things waiting on the other side of this life. Winnie talked to him about Nashville. She spoke about her brother Johnny once. A lot of nights she didn't come to the woods at all. On some of those nights, he could hear her screams echo through the trees.

But in all those years, never, not once, did Eli hear her speak about her daughter.

He hoped Walker's and Alva's love for that child would be enough. He hoped Walker truly was the new man he was trying to be.

But Eli watched all the same. Because little Hadley Dixon was living in a house built on crooked beams.

1989

Eli had been tending the grave of the copper-haired boy in secret, struggling every day with the right and wrong of the choices life puts in a body's path. He didn't know what to do.

Eli tried to comfort his mother when Winnie chose to leave the world in a rush of flames, just months after he'd buried the boy. Alva had lost another grandson who'd never drawn a breath. Before the night was done, she'd lost a daughter-in-law as well. She was terrified she was losing a son too.

"Walker said this was the last time. Said he wouldn't let her try for any more babies. That it was too hard to lose them all, one after another," Alva whispered. "He told her to hold tight to what she had. That it was enough. But I guess it wasn't."

Alva sobbed into her hands.

"He's gone, Eli. Disappeared into the barn with a bottle of whiskey. I'm afraid we won't ever get him back. How does a man come back from a thing like this?" she'd asked.

Eli didn't offer his mother any answers because he only had one. *Broken. Walker's broken, and he has been for a long time. He killed that boy. I can't hardly even stand to look at him, and now those broken pieces that are all that's left of my brother are gonna be crushed into dust.*

And he was right.

33

Jude stood, wiping the pear juice from her fingers on a kitchen towel. She looked churned up. Without a word, she took the empty tea glasses and walked back into the house.

The thought crossed Hadley's mind that she should get up and walk away now, while she still had the chance, like she should have done by the river. But she was kidding herself. She'd never had that chance. It was an illusion, and she was tired of the lies.

Jude came back with two fresh glasses. She handed one of them to Hadley and took her seat again, next to her friend.

"Three days after your mama died, I came to see you. Mama Viv sent food. Jambalaya, I think, and a casserole of some kind. I remember the basket was heavy. You were inconsolable. Hardly speaking. You looked right through me. Mama warned me you'd seen a terrible thing, and I shouldn't expect you to be acting like yourself, but it scared me all the same. It was like someone had left the lights on and the doors open, but no one was home.

"I didn't stay long. I just wanted to get back home."

Jude stopped. Then she took a deep breath and started again. "I was on my way there when Walker called out to me. I stopped and turned toward him, and he motioned for me to come closer. I never gave it a second thought. It was Mr. Dixon. I'd known him my whole life. He was my best friend's daddy. When I got closer I could see he didn't look the way he normally did. But none of you looked right.

"Your daddy, he looked like he'd slept in his clothes, if he'd slept at all. He smelled bad, like sweat and animal, and another smell I couldn't name. It was years before I realized it was the smell of whiskey. 'Hey there, Jude,' he said, like I'd stopped by after school to see you. Like it was any old day."

Neither woman looked at the other. One was looking into the past. The other at the pit that was opening up at her feet.

"He pulled me to him. I remember I dropped Mama's basket in the dirt. He slid his hand over my mouth and he told me not to make a sound. Not even a peep. Walker Dixon pulled me into that barn with him, and he raped me. Your daddy raped me, Hadley."

Hadley had taken a hot-air balloon ride once, in college. Once they'd risen high enough, the details of the world below became fuzzy, and Hadley's eyes were forced to refocus to take in the larger shapes and patterns made by the roads, the fields, and the houses scattered below. She felt the same sort of vertigo now. As if she were rising in a balloon above her life, only to see she'd been living inside a pattern of strange crop circles she'd never known existed.

"Excuse me," she whispered. She ran past Vivienne, through the Monroe house, and into the bathroom, where she vomited until there was nothing left inside but a dull weight that wasn't going anywhere. Hadley leaned her head against the wall. She had no idea how long she sat there. Long enough to count the tiles on the floor. There were fifty-seven, including the ones beneath her and the partials along the back wall. She should know—she counted them at least a dozen times. She couldn't stay there forever. Eventually, someone would come looking. And besides, she couldn't stomach her own self-pity any longer.

Get your ass off the floor, Hadley, some irritatingly rational corner of her brain said.

Oh, fuck you, she thought back. But she got up all the same.

34

"Did you know, back then?" Hadley asked Vivienne. Jude was in the kitchen refilling glasses that were still full and gathering her thoughts.

"I knew enough. I didn't know who, or why. I thought I did, but I was wrong. I wasted a lot of good hate on the wrong man."

The question was there in Hadley's face for Vivienne to see.

"I thought it was Eli, of course. I went to school with those boys, and Eli was always a strange one, even before he came by those scars."

Vivienne sighed. "But when it came right down to it, it didn't make much difference who'd hurt my baby. I know that sounds crazy, but it didn't matter if it was Eli, or Walker, or the man in the damn moon. The result was the same, and it took everything I had to get us through those days. Everything Jude had too, and then some."

Vivienne's eyes were on her daughter as she walked back toward them.

"That girl has strength in her, all right. Right down to the bone. She gets that from her daddy."

Hadley glanced up at Vivienne's profile. She wasn't so sure about that.

"My God, that day . . . I'll tell you the truth, that was the worst day of my life, and I mean that sincerely. Even the day I lost Joseph, at least I knew he'd been on the Lord's good side and he'd be at peace. But Jude? I didn't know if she'd ever find peace again."

Vivienne met Hadley's eyes, with shades of old pain on her face.

"It's a monstrous thing, Hadley, to be a parent. To see your child hurt and be powerless to mend it."

1989

When Vivienne found Jude she was huddled by the back door, trembling and mute. Her clothes were torn and dirty, her cheeks pale. Vivienne's breath caught at the confusion and pain she saw in her daughter's eyes, set in such an expressionless face.

Vivienne knew that look. Knew it all too well, and she knew the acts that had put it there. The eyes gave it away.

Gathering up her daughter with gentle hands, she held her close to her heart, while memories of the day Jude was born flickered across her mind.

She'd grown so fast. Some days it was too easy to forget that Jude was ten years old. Only ten. A child, a baby, shattered and shaking in her arms. She wasn't the same little girl Viv had sent out into the world a few hours ago. She never would be again. That child was lost. It was a loss she didn't have the time to mourn.

Vivienne took Jude, who stayed silent and still, into their home. She carried her as delicately as fine bone china. The baby in her belly, whose time was close now, rolled once between them, like he could sense the distress in his outside world. Then he settled into a stillness of his own.

Their house, which was never quiet, was strangely silent for once. The three older boys were with Joe, visiting his mother, and the baby was napping in his crib.

Vivienne began to sing to Jude, without noticing. It was "Silent Night." When Jude was born it was the only song Vivienne could remember the words to. It had soothed her daughter then, through colic and teething and hunger and growing pains. Joe thought it was so ridiculous he'd bought her a songbook of lullabies for Christmas that year.

It wasn't wasted. Viv put those songs to good use when the boys came later on, but by that time Jude had learned to associate comfort with the Christmas carol, and nothing else would do.

Vivienne carried Jude into the bathroom, then let loose of her just enough to peel away Jude's ruined clothing, and then her own. She ran a bath with her free hand. The water was warm and soapy when she stepped in with Jude still in her arms, cradled against her.

Gently, she bathed her daughter, trying in the only way she knew to soothe the nightmares that had come to life. When the water grew cool, Vivienne rose with Jude, wrapping herself in a towel and Jude in her own old terry robe. She carried her daughter to her bed and lay down next to her, wishing she had the power to make it all go away.

Somewhere along the way, as Vivienne stroked Jude's hair and quietly sang "Silent Night" again and again, Jude's eyes drifted closed and she slowly fell into sleep. She never made a sound.

Vivienne stayed with her for what felt like hours but surely couldn't have been. When she heard the baby stir in the room across the hall, she slid from the bed, tucking Jude in as tightly as she could before she slipped out of the room.

Viv traveled through the rest of the afternoon in a daze, seeing to the tasks that accompanied a family of seven and a half. She noticed none of it. She was grateful the baby was happy to play on the living room floor while she waited for the fractured thoughts swirling in her head to settle into some kind of order.

She looked in on Jude often, knowing she'd likely still be asleep. She was, but Viv needed the reassurance of seeing her chest rise and fall.

By the time Joe and the boys got home, she was running on empty, slipping dinner out of the oven and throwing out a distracted smile now and then. When Jude's brothers asked after her, Vivienne said, "She's come down with something. I sent her to bed, but you boys don't disturb her, now."

She hadn't planned the lie, but she knew whatever had happened to her daughter, the boys would never understand. She had no choice but to wait until everyone was in bed to break the news to Joe.

Somehow she made it through dinner, bath time, story time, and bedtime. All the while, her eyes were drawn to her husband. Joe was a good father. She was proud her children would never have cause to doubt their worth in his eyes.

Joe checked in on Jude himself. Vivienne was tucking Matthew into bed in the room he shared with the baby when Joe spoke from the doorway.

"She's out like a light. She looks pale," he said, with both a doctor's and a father's worry in his voice.

"Mama, is Jude okay? She promised to take me crawdad hunting," Matt said, his little brow furrowed.

"Jude's going to be just fine, champ," Joe said, but Matt looked at his mother for a second opinion, so she smiled and nodded, glad to be some comfort to at least one of her children.

"Of course she is, big man. She's going to be fine. She just needs a little time."

Matt nodded and snuggled into his pillow. Vivienne kissed his cheek and turned out the light, praying her words were true.

Later, after the children were all asleep and she lay in bed next to her husband, Viv knew the time had come to tell Joe what she knew in her heart to be true.

Their only daughter had been raped.

As they had gone about their nightly routine, Joe talked about the visit to his mother and his plans to take the kids to the county fair the next week. Vivienne hadn't heard any of it. Instead, those words had flown around in her head.

Raped. Daughter. Only. Their. She struggled to force her lips to form the sounds that would make it real. And then those moments slipped away. Before she knew it was happening, she found herself lying next to the sleeping form of her husband while he gently snored. The words were still locked inside of her like little house wrens, fluttering in their cage.

Quietly, she slipped from the bed, leaving Joe to his rest. Checking first that her daughter was still sleeping, she wandered aimlessly into the kitchen, her hands automatically going through the motions of making coffee. Pouring herself a cup in her old, chipped mug, Viv moved to the front porch swing, taking the afghan her grandmother had made for her when she was expecting Jude.

Only then, with the stars peeking through the treetops and the night sounds surrounding her, did it occur to Vivienne that she might have made a mistake bathing Jude and letting her slip into sleep, rather than immediately calling the police.

But she rejected those thoughts. A mother's need to protect her child is an ancient, living thing that defies rationality. Like Stonehenge or Machu Picchu, it simply is, and Vivienne felt no need to justify it. She couldn't fathom subjecting Jude to the questions of strange men in uniform, much less examination by doctors. Worse still if the doctor in question was the girl's own father. The thought of Jude's fear if she were forced to endure that kind of scrutiny sealed Viv's belief that calling the authorities wasn't an option. Not today.

If at some point Jude wanted to do that, they would cross that bridge together. But she wouldn't force her down that road. Vivienne's responsibility to her daughter was deeper and much more personal. And then there was Joe. Vivienne knew with every part of herself that had ever answered to the word *wife* that she should wake him up. She should do it now. He should know their daughter had been hurt. What right did she have to keep it from him?

But she didn't. Throughout the long night, she searched for the answer. Eventually, she accepted that, regardless of whether she had the right to or not, she wasn't going to tell Joe. It would bring so much pain, and in the way of men, especially good men, he'd have a need to hunt down justice for their girl.

Vivienne doubted justice would be an easy thing to find. It was a fine idea, full of principle and lofty intentions, but it was expensive. The payment demanded was the damaged self of a young girl laid bare for public consumption. That was a price she could never ask her daughter to pay, and it was a thing she could never ask her husband to let go. It would eat him alive.

Vivienne had never before been forced to pit her role as a wife against her role as a mother. She sent a silent apology to her husband, and to her God, both of whom she'd spoken her wedding vows in front of. But there was no comparison.

That was when the tears came. She endured their pain as silently as possible so she didn't disturb her family.

Her decision made, and resigned to the knowledge that her grief could help no one, Vivienne dried her tears. Then she slowly and painstakingly picked up the pieces of her heart and forced them back into place.

As dawn was breaking, she rose to face the day. Her daughter was going to need her.

35

Hadley was overwhelmed by shame. Her hands were covering her face and she was doubled over, rocking back and forth. She was too numb to cry. She should have known. She should have been able to warn her friend, to save her somehow. But she was years too late. How could she not have known?

Had she not wanted to see?

Viv held her, rubbing a hand across her back, as she tried to come to terms with the truth.

"Why, Jude? Why didn't you tell me?" But even as she asked the question, Jude was shaking her head. Hadley knew the answer.

"Hadley, I couldn't. I was so messed up. We were kids. You'd just watched your mother light herself on *fire*, for Christ's sake." Jude was visibly shaken, upset for both of them, for the children they'd been. "I had more than I could handle trying to put myself back together again."

"We lost each other," Hadley said, remembering the pain of surfacing from what felt like a hundred-year sleep to find her world had changed around her in fundamental ways she didn't understand. She had lost her mother, a baby brother she'd never had a chance to know, and her friendship with Jude. The loss of Jude was especially insidious, leaving a gaping, hollow place where her friend had always been.

"I missed you so much, Hadley," Jude said, her words running parallel with Hadley's thoughts. "I'd turn to say something to you. My mouth would be open and ready to speak before I remembered you were gone. Still here, still so close, but so far away."

"I did the same thing," Hadley admitted. "For years. It was like having a phantom limb."

"I'm so sorry, Hadley. I wasn't strong enough. I couldn't be close to you. Not just because of Walker." Jude wiped her palms on her jeans and stood. "I owe you an apology, Hadley. For a long time, I was full of anger."

"My God, Jude, you don't owe me an apology," Hadley said.

"But I do. I was angry because I couldn't understand how this could happen to me . . . and not to you."

"Jude . . ." Hadley absorbed the blow, accepting it as her due. "I'm so sorry."

"It's okay, Hadley. It's not your fault. It never was. But I was so confused. The years after that were hard. For a long time I felt alone and . . . dirty. Unworthy. I went back to school. I surrounded myself with people I called my friends, and all the while I blamed them because they never really knew me. Resented them because they weren't you. It was Eli who helped me get my head on straight."

"Eli?" Hadley asked. "I still don't understand."

Jude glanced at Hadley in surprise.

"It was Eli who found me . . . after. Eli was the one who brought me home."

1989

It was the crying that told him the world had gone to hell again. He'd been keeping an eye on his brother in the days since Winnie's death. He'd tried talking to him, but Walker looked right through him, his eyes blank. Not knowing what else to do, Eli searched the barn for liquor, but if Walker had a hiding place, Eli couldn't find it. So he backed off and left his brother to face his demons.

Still, he watched.

It was Alva who'd pulled him away. When his mother asked him, in a voice close to breaking with strain, if he could find the time to build a tiny coffin, he could hardly say no.

"Walker decided to have Winnie's remains cremated. I don't know if it's the whiskey talking or not. The idea makes me sick to my stomach, but he said, 'That's obviously what she wanted, Mama,' and what could I say to that? We'll just have to bury the urn."

Alva looked wild around the eyes.

"But I refuse to let anyone burn that baby."

Eli wondered if this was all more than his mama's mind could handle. If these past few days had done what even Silas couldn't do.

"You make me another casket, Eli. A simple pine casket to bury my grandson in. Just like you did the others. You'll do that for me, won't you?"

"Yes, Mama. I'll do that."

Alva nodded. The issue was settled.

Eli flinched when Alva brought a hand to his ruined cheek, caressing it like she couldn't see or feel the scars beneath her palm.

"Thank you, son," she said and walked away.

Eli checked on Walker first, but his brother was passed out drunk in the old barn loft. Eli took the ax from the barn that had been there since before he was born, and he went to find a pine suitable to cradle a baby boy in his grave. It was a terrible task, and one he'd done too many times.

Hours passed. It was when Eli was headed back to the barn to replace the ax that he heard crying. He started to run. Eli threw open the barn door. With the ax still gripped in his hand and backlit by the sun, Eli looked like the right hand of God, meting out the Lord's chosen punishments, razing cities on a divine whim.

Eli wasn't a man used to anger. His father's lessons had beaten that out of him. But seeing that beautiful child piled into a heap on the ground like so much dirty laundry caused a rage to rise in him like none he'd ever known. When Silas had nearly killed his mother, he'd known fear. When he'd buried the copper-haired boy, he'd felt an overwhelming sadness.

But when he looked at Walker, sobbing like a child who keeps breaking his toys, it was anger that pulled Eli forward. His heart raced and his breath shortened. He was overcome with disgust for this person in front of him, this person who destroyed the people around him. The children. The ones who least expected or deserved the pain.

Anger found Eli standing over his brother. He didn't know this man, sniveling and pathetic, at his feet. Anger raised Eli's arms, the ax held high above his head, poised to end it once and for all.

Anger brought the ax down.

The ax blade buried itself in the board behind Walker's head. The memory of the boy his brother had been, the first boy Eli should have saved, had turned his hatred back on himself.

It could have been mercy that stayed his hand. Maybe it was. Maybe it was his mother's eyes when she'd asked him to build a baby's coffin. It could have been either or both of those things, or a thousand others. But to Eli, it had the bitter aftertaste of weakness.

Eli turned to the child. His anger was gone, replaced with the knowledge that he'd failed again. He'd failed to protect this innocent girl from a threat she hadn't even known was there.

He picked her up, cradling her as gently as he had the dead body of her friend, and he did the only thing he knew to do. Eli took her home.

36

A week later Eli left the first of many small gifts at Jude's door. It was the basket she'd dropped, forgotten in the dirt. Eli returned it to her, filled with dark, hard pecans still in their shell. They were nestled on a bed of clematis vine that twined up and around the handle of the basket.

Vivienne was the one who found the offering, left there some time during the early hours of the morning. She recognized the significance of the basket, knowing exactly when she'd seen it last. It had been on Jude's arm the last time she'd seen her daughter's smile.

The basket of pecans could have come from Hadley or Alva, but Viv saw no reason why they wouldn't have announced themselves. The gift could have been from anyone . . . even the person who'd hurt her daughter.

In her heart, Vivienne believed that person was Eli. She couldn't know for sure. Jude had barely spoken in days. Vivienne told Joe and the boys Jude had womanly issues and to let her rest in peace, but Joseph was worried. Vivienne had put him off, saying, "It's part of life, Joe. She just needs rest until it runs its course."

But she was quickly running out of room there. This couldn't go on much longer. Viv had tried everything she could think of to get Jude to open up, to help her start to deal with this terrible thing. But nothing worked. Jude stayed silent.

Vivienne's first instinct was to get rid of the nuts, basket and all. To burn them, leaving no trace they'd ever existed. Maybe the gift was well meant, but the anonymity of the sender left her wary.

After staring at it for another beat, Vivienne reached down and snatched the basket up. She took it into the kitchen and put it in the pantry, hiding it behind canned goods and containers of rice and dried beans. She could throw it out later. Probably she would. Maybe.

Throughout the morning, while she saw to sending her husband and older children off with full bellies and packed lunches, the basket stayed on her mind. Once the day settled into place, Matt ran off into the backyard with his dump truck and one of his mama's best silver serving spoons to play in the dirt.

The baby made happy noises from his playpen, content with his bottle and his blankie. Jude was still in bed.

Vivienne held a cup of coffee that had long gone cold and stood at the screen door in the kitchen, staring with unseeing eyes at her son using pilfered silver to dig a hole in the ground.

Before she could change her mind, Vivienne went to the pantry and took the basket from its hiding place. Maybe it was nothing and she was overreacting. Or maybe it was a mistake.

She wouldn't know until she tried.

Vivienne opened the door to Jude's room and saw her daughter was awake. She was lying in bed, staring out her window at the clouds making their way across the sky. With a deep breath and a prayer that she wasn't doing the perfectly wrong thing, Vivienne moved into Jude's line of sight.

She set the basket on the little desk that sat in front of the window. "I found this on the porch this morning. There was no note, and I don't know who it's from, but I have to think it was meant for you."

Jude didn't react. She stared in the same direction, as if her mother had never spoken. Vivienne sat on the side of Jude's bed. She brushed her daughter's tangled curls away from her face. "I love you, Jude," she said. The words felt small.

Viv left her daughter to rest and checked in on the boys. They were so full of life. With a sigh, Vivienne sat at the table and laid her head on her arms. Then she heard a noise coming from Jude's room. She stood and moved down the hallway. She realized it was crying. She ran the rest of the way.

When Vivienne threw open the door to her daughter's room, she found Jude sitting on the floor between her bed and her desk. Her legs were crossed and the basket sat in her lap. She was sobbing into her hands, great choking sobs that seemed too big for such a little girl. Pecans had spilled across the floor.

Vivienne knelt and took Jude in her arms. She didn't notice her own tears or the hard brown shells around her. Only the relief that flowed, mixing and swirling with her sadness, when she heard Jude say, "I love you too, Mama."

37

Little gifts would show up on the porch now and then. Jude usually found them first, and Vivienne held her tongue. Over time, she tried to convince herself they were from Hadley, an homage to the friendship the girls used to have. Viv tried not to think deeply on that, for fear she'd notice the cracks in her reasoning.

She'd have been even more concerned if she'd known that her daughter periodically took a path through the woods that bypassed Hadley's house and visited Eli at his little shack. The first time had been months and months after the basket of pecans had shown up at their door. Entire seasons had been and gone.

Jude had knocked on Eli's door, nervous and shaking. Somehow she'd made it through the end of the school year, though it was all a bit of a blur. Hadley hadn't come back to school after her mother's death, and Jude had trouble sorting through her feelings about that. She'd grasped on to the summer months, avoiding everyone except her family. Secretly, she was afraid that if people looked closely enough they'd be able to see in her face what had happened and they'd treat her differently, pull away.

But summer was dying on the vine, and school was about to start again. Jude couldn't hide forever. So she'd gathered her courage, and she'd come to the river. She knew if she could do this, she'd be able to face a new school year. At least, she hoped so.

After such an agonizing buildup, Jude found no one home. She was disappointed, but relieved too. She wondered if the act of coming here was enough bravery practice to help her go to school next month. Did it still count, even though she'd taken the long way around so she didn't have to face Hadley or Hadley's daddy and, after all that, Eli wasn't even home?

Jude turned to the river, watching it roll by in the sun, sitting low and sleepy on its banks. With a huff, Jude sat down on the grass—not knowing she was a matter of yards from her friend Cooper's grave—and wondered about her next move.

She had no idea she was being watched.

Eli had seen the little girl coming down the path. It looked like she was coming to see him, but he could hardly credit it. No one visited Eli on purpose except his mother and his brother. Eli didn't call out. He hoped when she found his cabin empty, she'd head back in the direction she'd come from. He'd follow her and make sure she made it safely home.

But then the girl took a seat on his riverbank. He waited and watched, but she didn't look like she was in any hurry to leave. Eli didn't know what to do. Clearly, she'd come to see him. The idea made him feel awkward. Even Winnie had never come to the river looking for him. What could she want?

Jude would have laughed if she'd known this big, strange man had to dredge up as much courage to speak to her as it had taken for her to come. Eli didn't approach. He stayed in the shadows, wishing for the darkness of night to hide himself in. He was afraid, more than anything, that she'd be frightened of him.

Once he accepted that she wasn't going anywhere, he spoke.

"Hello," he said from the shelter of the trees.

Jude turned at the sound of his voice. The beam of a smile she sent his way threw him off.

"Oh, hello!" she said. Neither of them moved. Neither knew what to say next. Jude looked back at the river, seeming content to watch it pass in silence.

Eli, who hadn't moved, hoped the girl would go soon.

"I never said thank you," Jude said. "For bringing me home."

Eli was humbled by the strength and beauty of this child.

"No need," he said quietly, knowing he didn't deserve her thanks. He was to blame for what his brother had done to her as much as Walker was. The girl should be spitting at him.

"You okay, then?" Eli asked. He knew she'd never be okay. Jude tilted her head at the question, then spoke in a quiet voice.

"Not really," she said. "It's like a splinter in your foot. It's there even when you're not thinking about it. I've been trying real hard to pull it out, so it won't hurt anymore, but that's not working so well. So I think I'm just gonna have to learn to walk on it, even though it hurts."

Jude seemed to consider that for a moment, then her face cleared and she smiled at Eli again.

"Thanks for the pecans too. I cried a lot that day, but then I felt a little better. Mama taught me how to make pecan pie. My little brothers and my daddy finished it off in one night. Daddy said it was the best damn pecan pie he'd ever tasted. Mama got onto him for cussing at the dinner table, but I think it made her happy anyway."

Jude stood up to go.

"Next time, I'll save you some," she said with a smile.

There'd surely been stranger friendships, but not many.

Jude never spoke of Eli to her family or friends. Eli hardly spoke at all. But he grew more comfortable with her, over time, and eventually stopped worrying she'd be afraid of his scars and moved into the daylight when she came around.

He needn't have worried. Jude wasn't scared of Eli's scars. She'd learned that the scariest things around didn't look like a Halloween mask. They looked like your science teacher or the mailman, or your best friend's dad.

Whenever Eli came across something he thought Jude would like, he'd pluck it from the woods and leave it for her to find. Jude thought he did it to make a friend smile.

And he was glad to do that, if he could.

But every gift he left her was an apology, too. Because *sorry*'s just a word.

38

Jude was seventeen when Kyle Miller tried to take things further than she wanted to go, on their first and only date. She pulled away and told him to take her home. They were parked in a field near a keg party that was already in full swing. "Come on now, Jude. You know you like that. You don't have to play any cock tease games with me."

Kyle Miller believed that. He would have been surprised to know he was a date rapist in the making.

"Kyle, stop!" Jude said again, pushing him away a second time. "If you won't take me home, I'll catch a ride with somebody else," she said, reaching for the door handle of Kyle's car.

The date had been a disaster from the beginning, even before the high school football game or the postgame party. It started heading downhill when they caught an early dinner at the Mexican restaurant in town.

There was a Latino boy who'd been bussing a table next to theirs when he tripped and spilled dirty dishes across the floor. Refried beans and cheese splattered across the arm of Kyle's shirt. Jude felt bad for the boy. She rose from her seat and started to help him clean up the mess.

Jude didn't know she was making things worse. He'd tripped because he was too busy watching her from the corner of his eye to notice the chair that tangled up his feet.

He started to apologize to Jude in Spanish. He was perfectly fluent in English, but he was flustered. He'd looked up from the dishes he was scrambling to pick up to find the object of his year-long crush kneeling with him over the remains of table seven's *grande* platter.

"*¡Lo siento! ¿Está bien? Es la mujer de mis sueños,*" he said.

"I . . . I'm sorry, I don't understand," Jude said with a smile.

He'd just told her she was the woman of his dreams.

He was about to repeat his apology in English, except for the part where he confessed his undying love, when Kyle clued in to the fact that his date was more concerned with the busboy than his ruined shirt.

"Hey you," Kyle said. "Yeah you, kemo sabe."

Jude wondered if Kyle knew that *kemo sabe* wasn't Spanish.

"You've ruined my shirt, Frito Bandito. Think I could get a napkin over here to clean this off? Do you speak English? Speak-ay English-ay?"

A waitress was already headed their way, with a damp rag. She apologized and said their meals were on the house. When she took their orders, Kyle asked for the most expensive item on the menu. It was a family platter, meant to feed four. Embarrassed, Jude asked for water.

"I'll share his," she said to the young woman.

"Of course he speaks English!" Jude hissed once their waitress was gone. "His name is Mateo and he goes to school with us. He's friends with my brother!"

"Really?" Kyle asked, surprised.

"How can you not know that, Kyle? There are less than eighty kids in our whole school! And what does it matter if he speaks English or not? You still shouldn't talk to people that way!"

Kyle didn't appear pleased about being lectured, but he was smart enough to keep his mouth shut. When the waitress came back, Kyle even offered an apology for acting like a jerk. Jude noticed he didn't seek Mateo out to apologize, though. And he didn't offer to pay for their food either.

Things hadn't gotten any better after that. Kyle dropped Jude off at the game so she could join the other cheerleaders on the sidelines, but after the game was over Jude hesitated when he found her. She was having second thoughts about the party. He managed to sweet-talk her into it, but now she regretted it.

Kyle was clearly losing his patience. There she was, with her hand on the door handle, and he'd barely made it to first base.

Kyle made his worst mistake of the night when he reached out and grabbed Jude to stop her from getting out of the car. "Come on, baby, just let me get you warmed up, and you won't be able to resist."

He held her down against the seat of the car and climbed on top of her, forcing his mouth against hers and his hand up her skirt.

Jude had had enough. She snapped, punching and kicking at anything she could make contact with. She didn't waste time screaming, focused only on getting the body on top of her off. Her fists and knees found their targets. When Jude climbed out of the car she was fighting off panic. She left Kyle Miller with a bloody nose and clutching his balls while moaning in pain.

Jude glanced around. She could hear the sounds of the party but couldn't face tracking down one of her friends in the crowd. Instead, she walked nearly two miles down the rural road to the nearest gas station. Each time she saw headlights she stepped back into the trees. She didn't want to draw anyone's attention, especially Kyle Miller's.

When she got to the Texaco station, she used the pay phone in front of the store to call her mom, asking her to come and pick her up. When Vivienne arrived there was worry all over her face. "Thank you, Mama," Jude said when she got in the car. "I'm okay. I'm not hurt. And I don't want to talk about it."

Vivienne opened her mouth to say something, but the set of her daughter's face must have told her it wouldn't do any good.

Jude took a long, hot bath, then went to bed, but she tossed and turned, unable to fall asleep. In the early hours of the morning, she gave up.

Jude knew if she woke her mom, Vivienne would make coffee and sit at the kitchen table with her while she cried or railed or howled at the moon. She also knew her mother's eyes would fill with worry and she'd try to fix things for her. But if Mama could fix her, she'd have been fixed a long time ago.

Jude didn't want pity, or worry. She didn't know what she wanted.

It was nearly dawn and her parents would be up soon, so after she got dressed she left a note in the kitchen. *Gone for a run, be back soon.*

And she went to find Eli.

"Don't you ever sleep?" she asked when she found him sitting outside his home on an overturned bucket, carving something into a lump of wood with a small knife. The sun was starting to stir, warming up for its big entrance. Jude wondered how he didn't slice his fingers off, playing with knives in the dark like that.

"You made so much noise I woke up," he said. Jude thought that was probably a joke, but she couldn't be sure.

"You okay?" Eli asked, like he did each time they spoke. Usually, she answered, "Yeah, sure," or "Okay enough," but this time she didn't.

"No, I don't think I am," Jude said, pulling up an old plastic milk crate and taking a seat. Eli kept whittling away at whatever was in his hand and waited.

Jude hesitated. This was why she'd come, wasn't it? To have someone ask her if she was okay?

"You know those pictures of the missing kids they put on the back of milk cartons? I keep thinking I'm going to see a picture of myself on one of them. I'm a missing person, Eli," Jude said, then cringed at her words. She sounded so dramatic and self-absorbed, but Eli never seemed to judge her. Sometimes he didn't even reply. Like now. He waited for whatever would come next.

"When I'm with somebody, I pretend to be whoever I think they want me to be. My friends, my family, strangers, it doesn't matter. I've done it for a long time. It's easier, you know. I learned how to read the cues in their eyes. And it worked. The problem is, I don't think the real me is in there anymore. I've gone missing."

Eli didn't say anything. He just kept carving his wood, little curly slivers falling to the ground between his feet.

Jude was frustrated with Eli's silence.

"Well, aren't you going to say something?" she asked.

Eli glanced up at her. "If you want."

"I do want. I want very much."

"You're not gonna like it."

Jude gave a snort. "Yeah? Well, hit me with your best shot, O Wise One."

Jude's attitude was wasted on Eli, and she felt small for being ugly to him.

"That's a load of bullshit," Eli said. Jude didn't feel so bad anymore.

"Excuse me?" she asked.

"I said, it's a load of bullshit," Eli repeated, a little louder this time.

"What exactly is that supposed to mean?" Jude asked, wondering why she'd ever thought Eli would understand.

"It means you're not missing, girl." Eli leaned over his piece of wood and blew away the last shavings that clung there. Then, as the sun was starting to light up the day, he handed over what he'd been working on. It was crude, not the skilled craftsmanship of the carvings on the trees that surrounded them, but Jude recognized the form of a little wooden bird.

"A mockingbird," Eli said. "Borrows his song from what he hears around him. But you ain't no bird."

Jude stared at the tiny figure in her hand.

"You ain't no bird," Eli said again, clearly thinking she didn't understand. And she didn't. "You're a girl," he said slowly when Jude looked up at him in confusion. "You got your own song. You ain't been listening to yourself. You're scared. Scared people gonna see your scars, like me."

Eli stood up and brushed the wood shavings from his lap.

"You got to listen better, girl. Or you gonna end up hiding in the woods your whole life."

2012

"After that, I taught myself how to stand still and listen closer, like Eli said. And he was right, it was bullshit," Jude said.

They were still sitting on Vivienne's porch. They watched as Mateo and Kate pulled into the drive and unloaded gallons of paint from the truck. "I am so sorry," Hadley whispered.

"Okay, stop right there," Jude said. "That is the last time I want to hear you apologize for something you had nothing to do with. This, all this cutting open the past like an autopsy . . . It's not about making you feel bad. It's not about you at all. Or me. It's about that little girl over there getting ready to paint my mama's house purple."

"It wasn't Eli in Kate's room," Hadley said. It wasn't a question, but Jude looked at her anyway and said, "No, it wasn't."

39

"I should have told you years ago."

Jude and Hadley were headed back to the hospital. The doctor had called. Alva was awake.

"The truth is I didn't want to face it." Jude was driving. She carefully kept her eyes on the road.

"I dealt with the past in the best way I knew how. I buried it. Mateo knew. But I never told him who. Him or Mama. Not until the night before last. I thought it would be too hard for him, knowing Walker was right down the road. He didn't have the years of practice I did at pretending it had never happened." Jude sent Hadley a small smile.

"I can't claim it was the healthiest way to deal with it, but it worked for me."

"And then I came back," Hadley said.

"Then you came back," Jude agreed, "with Kate."

Jude sighed.

"I didn't know about Cooper. Not until Eli came to me a few nights ago. But that's no excuse. I knew enough." She sighed. "Eli watched over you, you know. For years. He saw how you were with Walker, and how he was with you. When you moved back here, he watched Kate too."

"How did he know Kate wasn't safe?" Hadley asked.

"He told me that when Walker talked about Kate he said all the right words, but he wouldn't meet his eyes."

"And that was enough?" Hadley asked.

"Enough for him to worry. Enough for him to watch. It could have been a coincidence that Eli was outside your house night before last. But I don't think so. Afterward, he came to see me."

Eli had been returning his mother's dishes, planning to leave them for her on the porch. He'd been doing it for years, and it was an easy excuse. He'd been finding reasons to be near the house since the girl moved in. The reasons were becoming thin. He was running out of time.

Eli was watching the window to Kate's room as he walked down the path. He saw when the light opened in her doorway. Someone was standing there. He could make out a silhouette. It could have been Hadley or his mother, checking in on the girl, but Eli couldn't be sure. He set the dishes on the ground and walked closer to Kate's window. It was Walker. He was sitting on the edge of Kate's bed. His hand was stroking her hair.

All the years that had passed since he'd chosen to let Walker live were for nothing. It didn't matter that he hadn't seen Walker take another drink since he'd buried that ax next to his head. None of it mattered.

Eli's fist came up and banged on the glass of the window. Walker looked up into his eyes. Eli thought he saw fear there, but it was too dark to know for sure. He watched Walker stand, then leave his grand-daughter's room. Eli's legs wouldn't move. He stood there and asked forgiveness for the terrible mistakes he'd made. Maybe God could find it in his heart to forgive him, because he'd never forgive himself. He heard the sound of a truck start. Walker was running.

Eli couldn't keep his brother's secrets any longer. He needed to talk to Jude. He needed to warn her. And he needed to do it now. Because Walker's secrets were Jude's secrets too.

40

When Jude and Hadley made it to the hospital, they found Gran weak, but she seemed glad to see the two women. She didn't try to speak under the oxygen mask that covered her mouth and nose, but she squeezed Hadley's hand and gave them a ghost of a smile.

The doctor said her prognosis was good. They'd stopped the bleeding before major damage was done, and with time and care, she could make a full recovery. He told them about some of the side effects they should be prepared to see. Jude and Hadley glanced at one another when he mentioned possible damage to her short-term memory.

Only time would tell how much her grandmother remembered of the day before. Hadley avoided speaking of her father. Instead, she talked to Gran about Kate's latest art project with Mateo. After that, she resorted to reading to her from the newspaper. Hadley's mind wandered while she read the words off the page without listening to them. She couldn't help but think of the life her grandmother had led.

Hadley thought she knew, now, why she had such a fascination with carousels. When Alva had first looked upon those busted-up horses left on the side of the road, she must have seen something broken that she could fix. Something abused and abandoned that she could restore to beauty.

When her grandmother closed her eyes and drifted off to sleep, Hadley couldn't suppress a sweet sort of envy.

To sleep now would be a fine thing.

Hadley kissed Gran on the forehead and hoped she'd understand what Hadley had to do next. Whatever that might be.

As they left the hospital Hadley asked her friend, "Jude, is there anything else I need to know?"

"Probably," Jude said. "But now you know everything I know."

Hadley nodded. "The question is, what do I do now?" She shook her head, then looked her friend in the eye. "The only thing I'm sure of is my responsibility to my daughter."

Jude stopped and caught her in a hug. "Whatever happens, just know that you and Kate won't be alone. You were right before. I wasn't there for you when you needed me. I couldn't be. But I am now."

Their arrival at Vivienne's house was anticlimactic. They could see through a break in the trees while coming up the road that no one was home at the Dixon house. Only Alva's old car was parked out front. Hadley tried not to obsess over where her father was or when he'd return. It would happen when it happened.

No one was home at the Monroe house either. Vivienne, Mateo, and Kate had gone into town for lunch, leaving a note on the kitchen table. Hadley wanted nothing more than to find her daughter and a safe place to hide. But she knew what she had to do.

"I have to tell her," Hadley said, staring out the window at Charlotte Abbott's house next door.

"I know," Jude said. "Do you want to do it now?"

Hadley nodded. "Before I lose my nerve."

"Okay, then," Jude sighed. "Let's go."

Hadley looked over in surprise.

"What?" Jude asked. "You didn't think I was gonna let you do this alone, did you?"

Hadley reached out and squeezed her hand.

"Thank you," she whispered.

The Abbott house was the picture of disrepair. Chickens clucked and scratched at the dirt in the yard, the only signs of life. Walking up the front steps, the women avoided a board gone soft with rot.

Hadley stood for a moment, looking at the front door. Then she took a deep breath and knocked. Nothing stirred except the chickens behind them.

Hadley had a horrifying moment when she was sure that Charlotte Abbott had died, alone in a house that no one came home to anymore.

When the doorknob turned, she half expected to see a dusty skeleton on the other side, motioning them to come in.

But the woman who opened the door was very real, if no less of a shock.

The outside of the house reflected the state of its sole inhabitant. Hadley had once compared Charlotte Abbott to bright silk, but time and loss had taken her color and her shine. In their place was a faded woman. Her once burnished hair had given in to gray and hung limp down her back. Her skin was pasty and plump, her dress a washed-out gray that might have been blue, a lifetime ago.

Sadness rang like a bell inside Hadley. "Mrs. Abbott?" she asked.

"Yes?"

"I'm Hadley Leighton . . . Hadley Dixon. I was friends with your son."

Mrs. Abbott's face lit up like someone had flipped a switch.

"Of course! My goodness, you're all grown up. And you're Jude, of course."

"Yes, ma'am," Jude said, a hint of a smile on her face.

"Well, come in, come in, girls."

The inside of the house was surprisingly tidy. There were no cobwebs in the corners, no dust on the mantel.

"Can I get you something to drink?" Mrs. Abbott asked.

Hadley and Jude looked at one another.

"Um, okay," Hadley said.

She didn't know what she'd expected, but this wasn't it. Jude shrugged her shoulders when Mrs. Abbott bustled into the kitchen. They took in the house that neither had set foot in since they were children.

With a start, Hadley realized everything was the same.

The furniture, the photos on the mantel, the curtains in the windows. A little more worn, the colors faded, just like the lady of the house, but otherwise identical.

Charlotte Abbott was living in an aging time capsule.

Their hostess came back with a tray of iced tea and slices of apple cake.

"It's so good to see you girls. Please, have a seat."

They sat side by side on the sofa while Mrs. Abbott took a seat in a chair.

"You two both grew up just as pretty as a picture. Tell me what you've been up to. How are your families?"

They glanced at one another again. Her welcome had thrown them off balance.

"Um, good," Jude said. "Daddy passed away five years back now, but Mama's doing well."

Mrs. Abbott nodded. "I'm sorry about your daddy, Jude. He was a good doctor and a fine man."

"Thank you," she said. "I'm married now. Mateo and I have a house just up the road. We own a restaurant. The Voodoo Queen."

"That's wonderful, dear!" She turned to Hadley. "And you, Hadley? Are you married too?"

"I . . . no. I mean, I was, but not anymore. I'm a widow, actually. I lost my husband in an accident."

"Oh, I'm so sorry. I know how hard that is."

Yes, Hadley supposed she did.

"Do either of you have any children?" Mrs. Abbott asked.

Jude shook her head.

Hadley was disoriented by the ease with which she asked the question.

"I . . . well, my . . ." *My father molested and murdered your son, and I'm really sorry about that. Can I make it up to you somehow?*

She shook her head.

"My daughter, Kate, and I just recently moved back here. We're living across the road with my family now."

"You have a daughter!" Mrs. Abbott smiled. "I always wanted to have more kids after Cooper. I would have been happy with a dozen, but it never happened. You should bring her by sometime."

"Kate?"

"Oh yes. I love to sew, but I've never gotten the chance to make anything for a little girl. How old is she?"

"She's eleven."

"That's such a sweet age," Mrs. Abbott said. "I remember when Cooper was near that age. So full of mischief. So sure he knew the answer to everything."

Hadley didn't know what to say. She looked at Jude for help, but her friend had none to give. Mrs. Abbott went on, oblivious to her guests' awkward silence.

"Would you like to see Cooper's room?" she asked.

Without waiting for a reply, she rose and moved down the hallway. They had little choice but to follow.

Hadley was shocked when Mrs. Abbott opened the door.

It was a boy's wonderland.

Shelves along the wall held toys, games, and shiny new sports equipment. A guitar was displayed on the wall. There was a television with what could only be a game system hooked up to it.

Hadley took in the books on the shelves. The entire Hardy Boys collection sat next to Orwell's *1984*. There were choose-your-own mysteries next to *Ender's Game* and Stephen Hawking's *A Brief History of Time*. Hadley ran a finger down a paperback copy of *The Catcher in the Rye*. The spine had never been broken.

"Wow," Jude whispered. She picked up a knight from the carved marble chess set that was set up on the desk next to a personal computer.

"Do you like it?" Mrs. Abbott asked. She opened the closet door, revealing a hockey stick hanging from the back of the closet door along with a Nerf gun.

"It's . . . it's incredible," Hadley said. Did people even play hockey in Texas?

The closet was packed with clothes. So many clothes that they formed a solid wall of fabric. Hadley saw they were organized from left to right, growing larger as they went. There appeared to be a man-size tuxedo tucked away at the very end.

"I hope Cooper likes it," she said.

Hadley met Jude's wide, stricken eyes. Jude turned away and carefully placed the white knight back on the board.

"When he comes back," Mrs. Abbott said.

"Yes," Hadley said quietly.

"Mrs. Abbott," Jude said. "About that . . ."

Hadley looked up sharply. She gave an infinitesimal shake of her head. Her eyes begged Jude to say no more.

Understanding, Jude looked unhappy, but she gave a sad sigh of agreement.

"Yes, dear?" Mrs. Abbott said, prompting Jude to go on. Jude's eyes moved back and forth from Hadley to the mother of the friend she'd lost long ago.

"I just . . . wanted to say . . . that I've never met anyone like Cooper. Not ever."

Mrs. Abbott beamed.

"What a sweet thing to say. He's going to be so sorry he missed you, when he gets home," she said, giving Jude a hug. She glared at Hadley over Mrs. Abbott's shoulder, but smiled again when she held her at arm's length.

"I still can't believe what a beautiful woman you've grown up to be. Your mother must be so proud of you."

The women said their good-byes shortly after that.

"Don't be strangers now," Mrs. Abbott said, waving to them from her open front door.

"What was that?" Jude asked in a low voice, as they walked back to Vivienne's house. Hadley shook her head. She couldn't meet Jude's eyes.

"I couldn't do it."

"Hadley, she deserves to know the truth."

"Do you think I don't know that?"

"Then why did we just have tea and cake and let her invite us back? Her son is buried less than a mile from where we're standing!"

Jude stopped walking.

Hadley turned to face her, but she still couldn't meet her eyes.

"I just couldn't do it," Hadley mumbled, looking down at her feet.

"Is this about your father? Are you protecting him, after everything he's done? After what he did to Cooper? To me? To your own daughter?"

Hadley's eyes flew to Jude's face. She could see anger and pain etched there.

"No!" she said. "No, I'm not protecting him! It's not about him!"

"Then what is it about?" Jude was close to shouting. They both were. Hadley flung her hand out and pointed back at the Abbott house.

"Were we in the same house?" she asked. "That woman has nothing left! Nothing! She's lost her husband, she's lost her son, and she's completely, utterly alone. All she has left is *hope*. That's all."

"Yeah, she's got hope," Jude said. "False hope. Her son is never coming back, no matter how hard she wishes it. She's got hope all right, but it's got nothing left to feed on. It's turned on her and it's eating her alive!"

"And what's the alternative? We hand her some bones in a box and say, 'Here you go'?"

"The alternative is the truth!"

Hadley knew Jude was right.

"Hadley, I know what it's like to spend your life hiding from the truth."

Hadley's voice was quiet when she spoke. "And I know what happens when a mother loses her last shred of hope. I can still see the flames when I close my eyes at night."

Hadley watched Jude's anger drain out of her.

"Oh God," Jude said. "What a pair we are. Do you think between the two of us, we have enough pieces left to make one whole heart?"

Hadley smiled through her tears. "I doubt it."

41

Hadley felt a tug of guilt at leaving Jude alone with a worried frown on her face, but she needed some time and space to think.

As Hadley drove through Whitewood, she passed the public library and the fire station. She and her father used to have lunch at the café. Walker had a weakness for their pie.

"Best damn slice of pie in town," he'd say, no matter the flavor. He loved them all. She must have heard him say it two dozen times if she'd heard it once.

She passed the Caddo County Sheriff's Department.

Hadley drove around aimlessly for a while. She was avoiding the inevitable. There were only so many paths forward. Each of them led to a dark place.

Finally, Hadley turned her car toward home, with her daughter on her mind.

When Hadley came up to the break in the trees that gave her a split-second view of the Dixon house, she spotted her father's truck in the drive. Hadley slammed on her brakes and the car fishtailed, gravel spraying from under the tires. He was home.

She forced herself to breathe—slow, deep breaths that did nothing to calm her heart hammering in her chest. She'd known this was coming. She'd known. She'd even thought she was prepared to face it. Now, though, she admitted she'd been hoping he wouldn't come back. That he'd disappear. Then she'd never have to see his face when his crimes were laid down, one by one, between them.

She couldn't stop the thought that if his love for her had ever been real, he would have stayed gone and spared her what was coming.

Hadley took a breath and started the car moving again. She turned into Vivienne's drive instead of the one that led to her family's home. The scene that greeted her brought her priorities into sharp focus.

There was Kate, with an oversize man's shirt over her clothes. She was speckled with pretty lavender splatters of paint. Even the dog seemed to have a little purple on her left ear.

Kate was laughing at Mateo, who'd painted purple paint across his cheeks and forehead and was making silly faces at her. Jude was seated on the porch swing. Her legs were crossed, one foot jumping like a fish on a line. Vivienne saw Hadley pull up and came out on the porch too, wiping her hands on her apron. She held a palm up to shade her eyes from the sun. Hadley could see tension in the set of her jaw.

Hadley joined them on the porch.

"He pulled in about an hour ago," Jude said. Her arms were around herself, her hands tucked in tightly under them. Hadley noticed her own hands were none too steady and pushed them into the pockets of her pants.

"Trying to keep Mateo here until you got back . . . it's been a struggle. Mama isn't helping either. She's ready to storm over there with him." Jude shot a glare at her mother, but Vivienne was unapologetic.

Mateo walked over to join the women. In spite of his antics with Kate and the ridiculous paint on his face, his jaw was tight. Hadley had hardly given a thought to the effect all this was having on him and Vivienne. But she didn't have the time or emotions to worry about that now.

"Thank you," she said to Jude. "Please, promise me you'll keep Kate here until I come back for her. No matter what."

"You're not going over there alone," Mateo said.

Hadley nodded her head.

"What if something happens, Hadley? You don't have to face him by yourself. Let us help you," Vivienne pleaded.

"You are helping, by keeping Kate safe. I have to do this alone."

No one looked happy about that, least of all Hadley, but Kate was headed their way. She met her daughter with a bright smile.

"The house looks great, Kate," she said.

"Thanks. Mateo says I'm a hard worker, and he should know because Mexicans are some of the hardest workers on the planet."

Hadley lifted an eyebrow at him. He shrugged.

"He told me I could be an honorary Mexican if I wanted, but I think he's messing with me. Don't you have to fill out paperwork for stuff like that?"

Hadley couldn't help but smile.

"Couldn't fool you, could he?" she said. "Hey, Katy-did, I have a few things to take care of back at the house, so how about you stay here and help Mateo finish up?"

"Sure," Kate said. "Tell Granddad I said hi."

Hadley hugged her daughter tight.

"I'll be back in a little while," she said.

She wished she knew what would happen then.

42

The house was quiet when Hadley entered. She wondered how many times she'd crossed this threshold. Thousands? Tens of thousands? Had the house always felt so much like a living thing, and she'd just never taken the time to notice?

The air fell down on her shoulders from the ceiling fans like a sigh. The dripping kitchen faucet was a pulse more steady than her own. There was a sadness here, in these walls. For the children it had sheltered. For the grown woman who stood here now, with the truth sitting like lead in her belly.

The clock on the mantel ticked away the passing seconds. Hadley listened for signs of life, but she heard nothing but the house that breathed around her.

The first step was the most difficult, the second only slightly less so. But she pushed herself forward, searching slowly from room to room. She checked upstairs first, then made her way back down. She could have called out, but she didn't, afraid to upset the balance of lives teetering at the edge of a cliff.

Her father's office, the last place she checked, was empty too.

He wasn't here.

Looking around the empty rooms, Hadley knew where she'd find him.

The barn door gave a slow creak that Hadley's nerves could've done without. Blinking, her eyes adjusted to the shift from sunlight to shadows.

Alva's horses were lined up like spectators for a show. The barn hadn't housed live animals for decades, and never in Hadley's lifetime, but the smell lingered. It had been absorbed into the earth, beneath the newer smells of paint and varnish, dust and farm equipment gone rusty from disuse. Another, less familiar smell made her nostrils flare. Liquor?

Her eyes scanned the inside of the barn, but she saw no one, not at first.

Then she spotted movement and her eyes swiveled, finding the source. He was sitting with his back propped against a beam, one leg straight in front of him, and the other knee up. As she watched, he took a swig of whiskey straight from the bottle, then leaned his head back against the beam. His eyes were closed.

Hadley riffled through her memories, but she couldn't bring to mind a single time she'd seen him drinking. Not even a cold beer with a buddy on a hot day.

By the time she realized she'd made a mistake it was too late. The memories ran free, flooding her.

She felt the excitement and anticipation as she saw him with yellow balloons for her eighth birthday. She felt the sting as he helped her dig gravel out of her palms when she scraped them learning to ride a bike. Saw his smile when she got back on, determined to learn. He'd run alongside her while the wheels were still shaky. Then suddenly she was out front, steady and leaving him behind, except for the sound of his laughter and shouts of encouragement.

She remembered the warmth of his arm linked in hers when he walked her down the aisle on her wedding day, and how it felt when she transferred the weight of her newborn daughter so carefully into his arms for the first time. She could see the tears in his eyes and hear the hitch in his voice all over again.

"Just as pretty as your mama," he'd said.

Each precious memory, stained and dirty.

"Hey, Hadley," Walker said, his eyes still closed.

Hadley was disoriented. The words and images that had held her prisoner for the last twenty-four hours painted this man as a child molester, a killer, a monster. She couldn't doubt the truth of them. But she was having trouble reconciling that with the man in front of her, the one she'd always known. His voice was the same, his face and form the same.

She walked closer, staring at him, desperately searching for some indication, some sign she'd missed because she hadn't known to look for it. She saw nothing. He looked like he always had. Like her dad.

An overwhelming sorrow stole her strength.

"Hey, Daddy," she said, sinking to the ground next to him. She leaned her head back against the same beam, her legs stretched out perpendicular to his. From this vantage, she couldn't see his face unless she turned her head. It was easier that way.

Minutes passed. Whiskey splashing in its bottle broke the silence. Walker brought it to his lips, taking another drink before he spoke.

"I've been sitting here fooling myself," he said. "Wishing I could change things, fix them somehow. Hoping things could be all right again. Eli told me—no more secrets. Time to make things right. For you. But I can't, Hadley. Things were never right. I was never right."

"Daddy, you hurt so many people." To her ears, she sounded like a little girl, asking her father to make it all go away.

"I don't deserve forgiveness, Hadley. I don't even deserve to ask for it."

Hadley thought of him sitting on the edge of his granddaughter's bed. She thought of Jude, broken and hurting. Of Cooper, who'd never had the chance to heal. Of Mrs. Abbott and the hope that ate away at her, alone in that house.

"You're right," she whispered.

Hadley heard the catch in his throat as he started to cry. She found she couldn't offer any words of sympathy, not with the faces of his victims still in her head.

"I tried to be a better man for you, Hadley. When you looked at me, you had this trust in your eyes. I wanted to be the man you believed I was." His voice broke, and Hadley was grateful she couldn't see his face.

"Then turn yourself in, Daddy," she said. "If you mean that, then face what you've done."

Walker didn't reply. The sounds of a grown man's choking sobs filled the barn.

Until the moment she'd spoken the words, Hadley had still been shuffling the possibilities in her mind. She could take Kate and run, leaving Gran and Jude, Mateo and Vivienne to do whatever they chose. It would keep Kate safe. But Hadley knew Kate wasn't her only responsibility, even if she was her most important.

She could send Walker away, beg him to go, if she had to. He could go anywhere, as long as it was away from here and the people she loved. But she knew that even if he went, she'd always be looking over her shoulder, wondering if he'd return. Wondering whose blood would be on his hands when he did.

This was the only way. Walker might never be able to atone for his acts, but he had to face the consequences of them. Knowing Alva and Kate would suffer when the truth came out was painful, but she couldn't see any other way.

"Hadley, honey, I love you. Even if those words don't mean anything to you now. And I wish I could be that man for you."

"Daddy, you don't have any choice. Either you make the call to Sheriff Hammon, or I'll do it for you."

"Honey, I need you to do something for me." Her father's sobs had stopped, and his voice was calm when he spoke again, as if he never heard her words. "Tell Eli it wasn't him. He wasn't the one who killed Silas."

"What?" she asked. "Daddy, what are you saying?"

"Eli hit him in the shoulder, before he passed out. But it was me. I heard the shot, and I found them. Eli looked past dead, but Silas was still alive, spewing filth and evil."

Walker's voice was cold now, clipped. "He laughed when he saw me. Laughed even with his shoulder bleeding, on his back from the pain. He laughed." As he spoke of his father, a lifetime of anger and hatred dripped from his words. "I hit him with the butt of the gun. Knocked the smile off his face. He was stunned, and I knew I couldn't let him get back up. I took that damn wooden leg off him. He'd use that leg. Use it to hurt me, when he felt like it."

Walker was lost in the past. Hadley wondered about his sanity.

"I took his leg, and I beat that piece of shit to death with it. Made sure he couldn't hurt us ever again. Couldn't hurt me ever again. Then I wrapped him in an old horse blanket that smelled like vomit and piss."

Walker trailed off, then took another drink from the whiskey bottle.

"I've never regretted it. But that boy, Cooper . . . your friend? I never meant for him to die. I'm not making excuses. It was still at my hands. He couldn't breathe, and it was too late when I realized . . ."

"Asthma," Hadley said, as grief stole the air from her lungs. "Cooper had asthma."

Hadley was filled with an overwhelming hatred for this man she loved. How could someone do that to a child? Cooper was just a child . . . and so was Walker, when it had happened to him. She was at war with herself.

"But Silas? I never lost sleep. I'd do it again if I had the chance. But I let Eli think it was him. I don't even know why. Guess I was in the habit of keeping secrets by then."

"You can tell him yourself," Hadley said. "Don't you owe him that much?"

"No need," came a deep voice from across the barn. "Knew already."

Neither of them had heard Eli when he came through the door Hadley had left open. Walker blinked at his brother, trying to make him out in the perpetual shadows that clung to him.

"All this time?" Walker asked.

"Blanket come undone when we threw him in the ground," Eli said. "Weren't no shotgun did that."

Walker nodded, accepting that.

Hadley wondered why Eli had kept this to himself, even when Walker's other secrets had come loose. Because sharing it couldn't help anyone? Didn't protect anyone?

Eli had never laid down the responsibility of being his brother's keeper. Wasn't that why he was here now?

"Hadley, you can head on inside. I'll be there shortly. We'll call Ben together, if you want. But I've got some things to talk over with my brother first." Walker's voice sounded so normal. There was no sign of the emotion or the liquor that must have been taking their toll.

Hadley stood, unable to break free of her role as daughter to this man. She'd do what he asked, this last time. No matter what else he was, he was still her father. How she hated him for that. Hated herself for the love she still felt for him.

As Hadley left the barn, she thought she heard him whisper, "I'm sorry, Hadley," but she could've been mistaken.

Hadley was sitting on the steps of the porch, staring at her hands. She jumped when the crack of a gunshot broke the day in two, sending the birds in the trees into panicked flight.

It didn't matter that she'd been waiting, listening for it. It didn't matter that she'd spotted the pistol early on, sitting on the far side of her father. Silas's pistol, a trophy he'd taken for killing a boy half a century ago, in a country far from home. It didn't matter that even as she'd spoken the words, she'd known in her heart that her father was too weak to face his crimes, even at her request.

Still, she'd hoped.

Hadley laid her head on her arms and let herself cry. She cried for her daughter, who was safe now. She cried for her father. And she cried for the loss of the man her father could have been.

That was how Eli found her a few moments later. He hesitated, then took a seat beside her.

"No other way," he said. The words had an empty, hollow ring to them.

"I know." Hadley's voice was low. "I just didn't think he'd have the courage, in the end."

Eli wasn't looking at her but at the figures running in their direction from across the road, the consequence of a single shot traveling at the speed of a heartbeat.

"He didn't," Eli said. Then he stood. Hadley watched as he made his way back into the trees.

43

Sheriff Hammon had his hat in his hands. He was standing in the Dixons' kitchen, looking uncomfortable and shell-shocked. He rolled the brim of his hat around his fingers, and his eyes roamed, looking for solid ground to land on. The more pronounced his discomfort grew, the calmer Hadley got. Ben Hammon had been friends with her father since before she was born.

They were alone. She'd sent the others back to Vivienne's house before she called the sheriff.

"Mrs. Leighton . . . It looks like suicide. I don't understand it . . . Walker? I'd never have believed it . . ." He stopped himself and Hadley could see him struggle with his role as a professional and his confusion as a friend.

Sympathy unfurled inside her. From all outward appearances, the sheriff was a good man.

Hadley wondered if she'd ever feel that way about someone without second-guessing herself again.

"I know how it looks, Sheriff."

"I just don't understand . . . why?"

This was her chance. Her cue.

"Hadley, I need to call this in and get an ambulance out here."

She'd bypassed official channels when she called Sheriff Hammon directly and asked him to come out to the house alone. There were procedures to follow and paperwork to do. The details that accompanied death.

The moment had passed by. Swallowing her shame, Hadley watched it go.

Three days after her father's death, Hadley was tucked into the ancient porch swing. She watched the sun rise, trying not to think of anything at all, only soaking in the light rising in the fog. It was quiet here.

They were putting Walker in the ground that afternoon. A private ceremony, at her request.

As the day started to gain definition, Hadley stepped back inside and set her mug in the sink. On a whim, she went upstairs to her closet and found the easel and paints she'd put out of sight. Downstairs, she slipped into an old pair of boots her grandmother always kept in the front closet. It had been years since she'd walked among the graves at the old family cemetery. That was where her feet took her now, leaving prints in the dewy grass behind her, marking her way.

Within moments, she crested a rise and saw the willow tree below, morning mist still clinging to the earth around it. Her breath caught at the beauty of the place, so still and calm.

She made her way down slowly, as if her presence might send ripples through the scene if she moved too quickly. She walked there, among the dead, studying the headstones more closely than she ever had as a child. She was struck by how few of her ancestors had died of old age. The older stones read mostly Erikson, the name of Alva's mother's family and the original inhabitants of the farmhouse that waited at her back.

The plot of land was small, thirteen graves in all. Winnie's headstone wasn't hard to find. There was a newly dug hole in the ground next to it, the rich dirt piled high and waiting. Hadley saw the four heart-shaped flagstones trailing among the grass and dandelions alongside her mother's grave. The larger stone was marked with Winnie's full name and the dates of her birth and death. Hadley was shocked to see she had only been thirty years old when she died, younger than Hadley was now.

Below the dates, the stone had been carved with an inscription.

MAY PEACE BE FOUND IN DEATH

Hadley knelt, running her hands across the words. Winnie Dixon and her lost boys.

She thought of Charlotte Abbott, who'd lost her boy too.

Hadley set her easel up below the tree and hoped for nothing more than to find her way out of the fog.

A while later, the sound of a truck pulling up the drive intruded, but she didn't turn away from the canvas in front of her.

When Sam walked through the field toward her, she concentrated on the viridian green, adding a little more yellow ochre to get the sun coming through the willow just the right shade.

"Hadley, I'm sorry," were the words he spoke. But the way he raised his palms, as if to comfort, then slid them into his pockets, said so much more.

But her mind—and, more to the point, her heart—was boxed in. They were squeezed between granite walls that pressed until she could hardly breathe.

"You should go," she said.

"Hadley, don't . . . Don't push me away. Not this time."

She shook her head, trying to throw off the words, like water droplets.

"Sam, I've got nothing to spare for you."

She didn't want to see his face. Didn't want to see the glimpse of a sunny fairy tale that was never going to happen.

He didn't go, though. Instead, he stood and watched her blend and push the paint across the canvas, absorbed the beauty of the movements.

Finally, he turned and walked away.

"The notebook that Cooper stole . . . the one full of bad poetry? Those poems were about you."

The brush in her hand grew still. But she didn't turn around.

"I can wait, Hadley."

"Don't," she said. "I'm not worth it."

Her brush began to move again. She didn't see him walk away.

Much later, Hadley walked back toward home. She had a funeral to prepare for. Leaving the graveyard behind, she heard an echo of song, dancing on the wind. It was a deep, sad baritone. Haunting.

It was singing the blues.

44

Hadley didn't sleep that night. After the unbridled terror of losing Charlie, even for such a short time . . . she was scared to sleep.

Something had cracked open inside her that day. If she let it, she was afraid it would crawl from its shell and eat her alive.

Or her children.

The morning dawned, in spite of her jangling nerves.

She took Kate to school, cherishing the sounds of her playing peek-a-boo with Charlie in the backseat. At fifteen, she'd be driving herself to school next year.

Time has a way of stacking moments on top of others, whether you're ready for them or not.

Then she went to see her friend.

"Doody," Charlie called.

"Can you watch Charlie for me for a little while?"

"Of course," Jude said. "Are you okay?"

She could have lied, but she owed Jude more than that.

"Not really. I have some things I need to do, though. Things I should have done a long time ago."

Jude stared hard at her face. There was plenty she could have said, but finally, she just nodded and gave Hadley the space she needed.

"Thank you."

Hadley was in the car, headed to see Gran, when she noticed the white steeple of the First Methodist Church standing tall and stately among the more pedestrian buildings of Whitewood. At the last moment, she turned the car in that direction. Gran was a long-standing member of the congregation there, but Hadley had barely given the church a thought in her adult life.

She imagined a black book somewhere with a tally of all the Sunday services she'd never attended and wondered if she could sneak in anyway.

When Hadley found the main doors of the sanctuary locked, she cocked an eyebrow at the sky.

"No fooling you, is there?" she muttered.

"What was that, dear?"

Hadley jumped and stifled a shriek.

"My goodness, I didn't mean to scare you," said the voice.

Hadley turned to find Mrs. Wainwright, her third-grade teacher, decked out in a floral-patterned gardening hat and matching gloves. She was holding a pair of shears that were so big they looked more appropriate for removing manacles from an escaped convict than dealing with the delicate pink rosebushes framing the church doors. They were nearly taller than she was. Hadley took an involuntary step backward.

"Hadley Dixon," Mrs. Wainwright said. "Oh my word, look at you. You're all grown up."

"Hi, Mrs. Wainwright. How are you?" Hadley asked.

"Oh, I'm fine, dear. Just fine. You remember my son Davey, don't you?"

Hadley nodded. "Well," Mrs. Wainwright continued, "he came out of the closet, oh, four years back or so. Took his daddy by surprise, that's for sure. But I can't say I was terribly shocked. A mother knows, you know."

The familiar way of small-town people, especially those who'd known her most of her life, could have been disorienting, but Hadley found it comforting. "Now he's married to a wonderful young man named Seth. They live in Colorado, so we don't see him as much as we'd like. They're hoping to adopt a baby soon."

"That's wonderful, Mrs. Wainwright," Hadley said. *Girls' hearts must have broken all over Whitewood that day,* she thought.

"Please, call me Julia. I'm retired now. But so is my husband, so I spend a lot of time helping out here at the church. Forty-eight years of marriage can start to circle the drain pretty quickly when you end up in each other's pockets for too many hours of the day."

Mrs. Wainwright's eyebrows drew together and concern clouded her eyes. Hadley knew what was coming next and braced herself for it.

"How's your grandmother doing?"

"Not great," Hadley said, shaking her head. "That's sort of the reason I stopped by."

"I'm so sorry to hear that. Alva's a sweet lady," Mrs. Wainwright said, subdued.

"I thought I'd visit the sanctuary for a little bit. Maybe light a candle for her."

"That's very Catholic of you, dear," Mrs. Wainwright said, some of the earlier twinkle coming back into her eyes.

"I'm kind of new to this," Hadley said with a shrug.

"Well, why don't you come with me, and we'll see what we can do."

The two women, striking in their dissimilarity, walked together around the church and went in through a side entrance. They made a detour into the church office, where Mrs. Wainwright exchanged her mean-looking garden shears for a rag and a can of lemon-scented furniture polish. She plucked a key from a set of hooks on the wall, and they continued on.

"The sanctuary used to be open to the public twenty-four hours a day, but that changed a few years back," she told Hadley. "There was an incident with old Mr. Mason. He wandered in without anyone noticing. Somehow he found his way back to the preschool classroom, where he ended up spending the night. Dementia," she said.

"It wouldn't have been that big of a deal, but he helped himself to some of the children's art supplies, and let's just say the subject matter of the paintings he left on the kids' easels was . . . inappropriate for four-year-olds."

"Oh my," Hadley said, trying not to laugh.

"It's okay, you can laugh," Mrs. Wainwright said with a smile. "There was some talk about auctioning the paintings off to help raise money for new playground equipment. Lots of interest, too. But the Mason family put the kibosh on that. Made a private donation to the church instead."

Larger cities have nothing on this place, Hadley thought.

"I usually make a pass through with some furniture polish before the Wednesday night service. I don't think Reverend Blackstone would mind if you keep me company while I do that."

"Are you sure?" Hadley asked. "I don't want to put you out."

"Of course I'm sure," she said, giving Hadley's hand a squeeze. "As long as you don't leave any pornographic paintings behind."

"I'll try to resist the urge," Hadley said, touched by this woman's help.

"Now, as for that candle. We don't keep shrines the way the Catholics do, but we do have the acolyte's candles around here some-where." Mrs. Wainwright rummaged around behind the altar in such a familiar way that Hadley had to stifle another laugh. She had an image of Jesus's grandmother licking her thumb and wiping a smudge of dirt from his face, then checking to see if he'd washed behind his ears before he was sent off to deliver the sermon from Mount Sinai. Or was that Moses?

The older woman emerged with a candelabra with a half dozen white tapers and a box of matches.

"I'll start with the pews in the back and give you some privacy. You take all the time you need."

"Thank you, Mrs. Wainwright," Hadley said.

"Julia, dear."

Mrs. Wainwright, whom Hadley would never be able to refer to as Julia, even in the privacy of her own head, was true to her word and left Hadley to her thoughts.

After such a fuss to get in here, Hadley found herself feeling small, dwarfed by the cavernous room that was empty of its usual bevy of parishioners. She took a deep breath and let the silence sink in. She watched the way the sun hit the hundred-year-old stained glass and felt the strength of the polished wood beneath her.

When it came right down to it, Hadley admitted to herself, she wasn't convinced God even existed. But in this place, surrounded by silence and beauty and history, she found herself hoping he did.

After a time, Hadley rose and made her way to the altar, her steps echoing in her ears. She lit a match on the edge of the box. The sound was magnified in the acoustics of the sanctuary, and the smell mingled with the scent of lemons. Hadley cupped her hand around the small flame and lit the first candle, sending up an unarticulated prayer for her mother, and the second, for her grandmother. Then she lit another for Charlotte Abbott, and one for Mrs. Abbott's son. With the match still burning, she surprised herself and lit another for her daddy's soul.

Hadley blew out the match, a little curl of smoke rising from the blackened tip. She turned to go, but then she changed her mind. She turned back.

Hadley lit one more match, one more candle, and sent up one more prayer. This one for herself, in the hope that she could find the strength she'd need to rattle old bones.

45

Hadley brought flowers when she visited her grandmother. Lilies and irises, elegant in their simplicity.

She knew the Alzheimer's had progressed. Gran was living more of her days in the past than the present. But those days seemed easier for her. It was when she was lucid, aware she was losing her grip on reality, that she got scared.

The nursing home where Gran had lived for the last year sat right off the square in the middle of Whitewood. Hadley stopped by the Rainbow Café first and picked up a few slices of fresh buttermilk pie, her grandmother's favorite. She was armed with flowers and pie. She also brought a package wrapped in brown paper. It was little enough, but all she had, save some raw emotions floating too close to the surface. Magnolia House was an old French Victorian that had once been the residence of the founding family of Whitewood. Now it housed up to ten residents, all in different stages of mental or physical decline.

The interior of the house had been modernized at different points over the years, eventually being outfitted with the necessities involved in caring for the elderly. The exterior was a different story. It had been lovingly preserved with all due attention to its original details. The effect was charming and peaceful, the house nestled in the shade of several magnificent century-old magnolia trees.

The scent of the blossoms filled the air as Hadley walked up the front path, wondering, as always, how to convey the feeling of a place on canvas.

The nurse said Gran had suffered a spell that morning, but she was calmer now.

She was seated in her room when Hadley arrived, her quilting frame set up in front of her. She was humming a tune as her fingers worked the needle and thread. Hadley knew right away that Gran's mind was in another time. Hadley smiled anyway, pleased to see her grandmother happy. She waited to see who Gran would like her to be today.

On her last visit, she'd called her Faye, the name of a girlhood friend.

"Hello there," Gran said graciously. "Have we met, dear?" So today Hadley would be a friendly stranger, stopping by for a visit.

"No, ma'am," she said to the grandmother she'd known all her life. "My name is Hadley, and I have two slices of buttermilk pie here that I couldn't possibly eat alone. Would you like to join me?"

Hadley spent the better part of an hour basking in her grandmother's gentle hospitality, a quality so deeply etched into her that even the grinding sands of Alzheimer's couldn't erase it. Gran might have lost her present, and her yesterdays were jumbled together like the contents of a child's toy box, but she would always have her charm.

It was a balm to Hadley's soul, one she badly needed. But then the visit took a strange turn.

Gran's eyes began darting from one corner of the room to the next, like she was afraid someone was sneaking up behind her. She held her hands tightly together, rubbing them occasionally, like she was trying to wipe something away that wouldn't fade. She looked so old then, so delicately frail.

Hadley's heart tightened. Eli would be building another casket soon. To lose Gran would be devastating. Hadley tried to put it aside. Gran was here now, and Hadley hoped to give her back some of the comfort she'd received.

"Gran," Hadley said.

Her grandmother's face swiveled and she met her eyes. "Faye?" she asked.

Hadley gave her a faint smile and led her to the bed. "Do you feel okay, Gran?"

"I . . . I don't know where I am." Hadley could hear the frustration in her voice.

"You're at Magnolia House, Gran. You've been sick. They're taking care of you."

Gran squinted at her, as if trying to place her. Like it was on the tip of her tongue. "Do I know you, dear?" she asked, her voice barely above a whisper.

"We met a long time ago," Hadley said. She couldn't cry. It would frighten her grandmother.

Gran nodded, but the wariness was still in her eyes.

Hadley had been holding on to a slim hope of explaining to her grandmother what she needed to do, but she'd put it off too long. She let that slip from her hands, and it floated away like a child's balloon. She would have liked a chance to ask, if not for her grandmother's permission exactly, then for her forgiveness. But the time for that had passed. Maybe it was for the best.

Hadley pulled up a chair.

"My name is Hadley, Mrs. Dixon. When we met before, you told me about your two sons."

Gran's smile broke through her confusion, brightening her face and chasing the fear from her eyes.

"My boys," she said. "Eli and Walker. They're good boys . . . Good boys."

"I brought you something. When I saw it, I thought of you."

Hadley rose and unwrapped the brown paper that protected the gift. The painting showed a river scene in watercolors, quiet and serene. On the bank of the river, with the sun shining on their hair, were two boys with fishing poles.

"Oh my," Gran said. "That is lovely. Why, it reminds me of my boys. Have you met my sons? Eli and Walker? They're good boys. Both of them. This is lovely, dear. Just lovely."

Hadley smiled through the ache inside. She had tried to convince Eli to come visit his mother here, but he always refused.

"Eli, don't you think she'd like to see her son?" she had asked him.

He'd shaken his head. "My face," he said.

"Eli, she's seen your face. She knows about your scars."

"Hurts her to remember. Forgetting . . . it's good." And he'd walked away.

"I'm glad you like it," Hadley said to her grandmother, then listened as Gran told her about her oldest son Eli's birthday party. She described the guests, the decorations, the games they'd played, the gifts he'd gotten. Every detail was recounted with pride. She only faltered when she spoke of the cake.

"We ate the cake with our hands," she said, and her gaze drifted away from Hadley. "Why do you suppose we did that?"

Hadley shook her head. "Maybe it tasted sweeter that way."

Gran's gaze returned to her, and her face settled. She could be content with that.

"Chocolate is Eli's favorite."

As Hadley listened to her grandmother talk about her boys, her frustration at Eli's stubbornness faded. She finally understood the gift Eli was giving his mother, along with the price he had paid for it.

46

Jude offered to come with her, and Hadley was tempted to let her. Jude had never been okay with the secrets, which had put a strain on their friendship. In the end, Hadley felt this was something she needed to do alone. When she thought she was ready, she knocked on Mrs. Abbott's door.

Hadley knew she'd cheated Charlotte Abbott out of justice for the death of her son. But she also knew that what Mrs. Abbott wanted was for Cooper to walk back through her door. Justice couldn't give her that. Nothing could.

Over the years that had followed Hadley's discovery of the hateful truth, she'd made regular visits across the road. Mrs. Abbott welcomed her warmly each time, and they spoke of Cooper often. What he'd be like now, what he might like for his next birthday or Christmas. How excited he'd be to see her again, once he made it home.

The visits were excruciating for Hadley. Each and every one of them. But she went anyway. She couldn't bear to think of Mrs. Abbott alone with her useless hope.

It was her way of doing penance for her own sins. Especially for her sin of silence.

She wondered now if she was doing the right thing. But Hadley had learned enough to know that there were some things she would never know. After all this time, she knew only that she needed to let Mrs. Abbott decide for herself. Seated in the same place she always sat, over iced tea in the same glasses, Hadley posed a question.

"Mrs. Abbott, I don't know how to ask you this without upsetting you. Please bear with me and know that I'm not trying to hurt you."

Charlotte Abbott tilted her head and waited.

"If you had a choice . . . a terrible choice between knowing what happened to Cooper so many years ago or holding on to the dream of him finding his way home to you . . . would you trade your hope for the truth, and the pain that comes hand in hand with it?"

It was Hadley's turn to wait.

Mrs. Abbott stood and moved to her mantel. She picked up a framed photo of the family she'd once had.

Finally, she said, "I would trade everything . . . *everything* to see my son's smile one more time. To hear him laugh."

She set the photo carefully back on the mantel.

"I've known for a very long time that was never going to happen."

She turned, and in a voice stronger than Hadley expected, she spoke again.

"My son is dead. He died on that October day. I don't know how, or why, but I know that death is the only thing that would have kept him from me for so long. My hope that he's coming home, the one I've clung to for all this time, that's nothing more than a reason for me to get out of bed. But it's an empty, worthless thing."

Hadley wondered if things would have been different if she'd been brave enough to ask that question years ago.

"So, to answer your question—yes, I would trade an empty dream for the truth. What do I care about pain? Do you think pain isn't an old friend?"

Hadley stood.

"Take a walk with me, Mrs. Abbott."

"Where are we going?"

"To your son's grave."

Ben Hammon had retired as sheriff two years before. He was a lifelong bachelor, and Hadley had heard he was spending his retirement building model ships in bottles. She supposed there were stranger ways to pass the hours.

"Sheriff Hammon," Hadley said when he answered the phone, the man and the title interchangeable in her mind. "It's Hadley Dixon." She'd long ago stopped bothering with her married name. Around here, she'd always be that Dixon girl.

"Ms. Dixon," the former lawman said, a question in his voice.

"There are things I need to tell you, Sheriff. You need to know where the bodies are buried, and I need to make things right. Can you help me do that?"

For a moment, silence stretched across the line, then Ben Hammon said, "I'll be right over."

It took months to navigate the murky waters involved in raising old bones.

After Sheriff Hammon started the ball rolling with a few phone calls of his own, Hadley found herself escorting a group of strangers on a silent walk through the woods.

"This is Cooper Abbott's grave," she said, indicating the patch of ground they'd come upon by the river. It was a serene place, remarkable in the amount of beauty that could be seen in a glance.

The ground was in bloom with wildflowers. Morning glory crept up the trunks of the surrounding trees. Everywhere the eye settled, there was another piece of loveliness to take in. A hint of bluebonnets peeking from the north, foxglove to the west, and the fresh, sweet blooms of honeysuckle and Shasta daisies to the south. To the east, the river made quiet music as it slowly passed by.

There were also carvings in the trees. Beautiful works of art depicting flocks of doves or a family of raccoons.

Someone walking past this spot might catch their breath, awestruck that nature had graced this little patch of earth with so much. But Hadley knew better. She knew this was a place tended daily with reverence and care.

When Hadley had brought Mrs. Abbott to this place, the older woman had fallen to her knees and wept silent tears.

"All this time," she whispered, "he's been so close."

Hadley couldn't speak. Her heart was in her throat. Her own tears were falling, dripping from her chin and soaking into the ground at her feet.

She held her arms tightly around herself and stood guard as a mother was reunited with her lost child.

"Why?" Mrs. Abbott asked. "Can you tell me why?"

Hadley nodded, wiping tears from her cheeks.

"I can. You deserve the truth, if you want it," Hadley said. "But it will never be enough."

"No. No, it won't. But I need to know."

So there by the river, near a cove where the fish liked to sleep, Hadley told Charlotte Abbot the story of her family and their sins, including her own. Sins that had stolen Charlotte's son.

Now the time had come for the river to let go of Cooper Abbott.

It seemed shameful to dig into the ground here, breaking open the earth and leaving nothing but a hole at the center. A sacrilege.

But it was time. Time for Cooper to go home.

"There's another one," Hadley said. She led the group to a darker, older place where the berry brambles were thick on the ground. This was the place Eli had shown her, when she'd asked.

"Never eat those," Eli had said, nodding to the fat, dark berries growing there. "Leave 'em for the birds, or to rot on the ground."

That particular warning wasn't necessary today, and she only said, "Careful, there are thorns in there."

Hadley found she was mostly in the way after that, so she stepped back and let the professionals who dealt in death do their jobs.

Statements were made, questions were answered, and the truth was brought into the light. Most of the truth, anyway.

Hadley never told Sheriff Hammon of Eli's involvement in concealing Cooper's death or Silas Dixon's. Maybe it wasn't up to Hadley to make that decision. Many might say Eli had plenty to answer for. But to her mind, he'd served his penance, and then some, for the choices he'd made. She wasn't about to give anyone a chance to say differently.

It was a decision she could live with.

What didn't sit as easily was the thought of the boy. The first boy Walker had targeted in the woods. Eli never named him, and Hadley didn't ask. He'd presumably be in his mid-fifties now. Possibly a local still, but maybe not.

Hadley couldn't get past the thought that there might be more. It seemed inconceivable that a man who'd started targeting children when he was in his early teens would have just the handful of victims they knew of.

What about the time Walker spent away from Whitewood? Hadley thought of the times her father had visited them when she lived in New Orleans. It was possible, probable even, that there were people out there whose lives had been . . . What? she wondered. Altered, ruined, shattered, set upon an unintended path?

Hadley knew she couldn't make amends to any of Walker's unknown victims. But she could offer the one thing in her power to give. The thing that had been denied them by the choices she'd made.

The same day Hadley called Sheriff Hammon, she sent a carefully worded document to the local newspaper, as well as the major papers in Cordelia and New Orleans. The story ran the next day in each one of them.

Jude told her she was crazy, but there was approval in her voice. Hadley could only hope that meant she was doing the right thing.

Locally, there were a lot of people who were appalled by Hadley's story. Shameful, they said. Airing your family's dirty laundry that way—it just wasn't done. But the parade of official vehicles coming and going from the Dixon farm was hard to miss. Whether the residents of Whitewood approved of her methods or not, there was no denying the truth.

She publicly declared her father, Walker Dixon, a child molester and a killer.

It would have been easier to leave it at that, but she found she couldn't.

The purpose of making my father's acts public is not to ask forgiveness for him. I cannot do that. Nor would I. These are sins that his soul will have to answer for. It is, instead, an acknowledgment. To those of you who are still out there. To those who have been hurt and who have suffered in secret and silence. You should know that you haven't been forgotten. That your pain matters.

For myself, I've found that love is a difficult thing to erase. I've accepted that this is my own sin to answer for. I cannot escape my family's past. I can only pray that those I love find peace, if not in life, then in death.

47

After months of waiting, the powers that be released their hold on Cooper's remains. In a pine coffin Eli built, Cooper Abbott was laid to rest in the Whitewood Memorial Cemetery, next to his father.

With Mrs. Abbott's blessing, Hadley had a small statue erected at the hauntingly lovely place where the river had sheltered Cooper for so long. It was a statue of a boy. A boy with an angel's wings.

After the small service, Hadley found herself sitting on the steps of her front porch with Jude at her side. Sam had come. She'd wondered if he would. She watched him play with her kids, listened to the way their laughter twined together.

Both women jumped when Eli appeared out of nowhere.

"Good lord, Eli! You can't go sneaking up on a person like that. I ought to put a damn bell on you," Jude said.

"Told you a long time ago, you need to listen better."

"Yeah, yeah." Jude waved him off.

Eli was standing with his hands in his pockets, staring off into the distance. He didn't look at either woman when he spoke.

"Come to say good-bye."

"Good-bye? Where are you going?" Jude demanded.

"Gonna follow the river. See where it goes."

"Where it goes? It goes to the Gulf of Mexico," Jude said, her voice rising.

"Then I'll see the ocean, I guess. Never seen the ocean," Eli said.

"And then what?" Jude asked.

"Don't rightly know," he said. "Guess I'll turn around and go back to where it starts."

Jude's mouth opened, but when no words came, she shut it again.

"Don't need to stay no more." He looked easy about it. Lighter.

And with that, he turned to go.

"Eli, wait," Hadley said. She walked up to his big frame and hugged him.

He went still with shock. Then he raised one hand and patted her twice on the back. Hadley hid a smile at his awkwardness, then released him, to his relief.

"You be careful, okay?" Eli nodded once, then turned again to go.

"Eli," came Jude's voice from the porch. He and Hadley turned back in her direction. But words failed her friend.

"I'll stop back by after I see the ocean," Eli said. "On my way upriver."

Jude nodded once, quickly, fighting off tears.

Then Eli turned and walked back toward the trees.

"That old fool is gonna get himself arrested for vagrancy and trespassing," Jude said, wiping at her eyes.

Hadley stood in front of the old farmhouse with one hand on her hip, the other shading her eyes from the setting sun, and watched him go. She felt a sense of wonder at his bravery. At his hope.

Her eyes were drawn back to Sam. He launched a stick for the dog. It arced through the air.

Hadley wondered if she could find some of that hope lying around.

Eli was right. This house had been built on crooked beams. But there was plenty there worth saving. Together they'd shored up what they could, then knocked down what they couldn't.

What remained was stronger for it.

A NOTE TO READERS

For all of you who've walked this far down the darkened path with me—thank you. Truly.

This is the place where I'm told I should hit you all up for reviews. But as much as I appreciate reviews, good or bad, I consider them a gift. Not an expectation. Never a requirement. I am, at heart, a lover of quiet. Of small, intimate stories told by a campfire. Of shared laughter over morning coffee while birds sing their secret songs to one another.

I'm here, in the quiet parts of the world. If you'd like, you'll find me at theelizamaxwell@gmail.com. I do hope you can drop by for a chat. My door is always open.

A NOTE TO READERS

ACKNOWLEDGMENTS

A big, sloppy thank-you to my husband and kids, for all the times you asked me questions and got nothing but a glazed look in return. It's a wonder you stick around.

Thanks to Katie Shea Boutillier, literary agent extraordinaire, for keeping the faith and having my back. Editors are the unsung heroes of the writing world, and I've been lucky enough to have the help of a few. Here's to the amazing talents of Stephen Parolini, Miriam Juskowicz, and Faith Black Ross. Please don't hold them responsible for the final draft; they tried their best to keep me in line. Thank you to Randy Gunter, who could have flunked me. Probably, he should have. But he chose to give me a second chance instead.

For those few brave souls who were my early readers, Kimberly Vaulkner Davis and Amy Tanner, a heartfelt thank-you.

Thanks to Trixi's dad, Paul Burwell, the original snail killer.

And last, but never least, Nicole Padilla. Those lunches keep me sane. Or sane-ish, at least.

ABOUT THE AUTHOR

Eliza Maxwell writes fiction from her home in Texas, which she shares with her ever-patient husband, two impatient kids, a ridiculous English setter, and a bird named Sarah. Her second novel was *The Kinfolk*. An artist and writer, a dedicated introvert, and a British cop drama addict, she enjoys nothing more than sitting on the front porch with a good cup of coffee.